A NOMAD
Repaints the Globe

A NOMAD

REPAINTS THE GLOBE

PREMJI

PARTRIDGE
A Penguin Company

ISBN: Hardcover 978-1-4828-1338-8
Softcover 978-1-4828-1337-1
Ebook 978-1-4828-1336-4

Partridge books may be ordered through booksellers or by contacting:

Partridge India
Penguin Books India Pvt.Ltd
11, Community Centre, Panchsheel Park, New Delhi 110017
India
www.partridgepublishing.com
Phone: 000.800.10062.62

Contents

Dedicated to

Johannes,
Founder and developer of www.poetfreak.com,
World's fastest growing poetry archive . . .

Foreword

I HAVE KNOWN PREMJI, this master of short-story writing for some years now and have consistently admired his ability to bring to international readers a unique feel of life as found in all kinds of phases. He writes in an easy accessible style but with quite an enigmatic depth which shows his objectives as always genuine.

Prem is unafraid to tackle any subject and is passionate about humanity's sufferance of inequity amid need for interpersonal relationships. He handles all subjects with compassion and finesse as in his story of—*'For your eyes only'*

The old woman embraced her with the strength of her strengths. Sometimes a touch is more powerful than millions of words.

Or his—*'Days of love'*

'Please don't cry . . . you may dissolve me away,' She hugged me tightly and planted a kiss on my lips.

Premji comes from a village in Kerala, India, where he teaches Engineering. His wife and young family feature in many of his stories as this caring author bases his writing on real life and tries to leave an uplifting lesson to end each story. This author is both compassionate and expressive in the hope that his readers might identify with some of the feelings each story highlights and find value to take away and long remember.

Perhaps his story of—*'Woman of Substance'*—states this best as a final example when we read that—'The finest language ever in the history of mankind is silence.'

Speaking three languages fluently, Prem has added painting to his long list of talents. It is my pleasure to be able to bring this volume to your hands.

Ms Fay Slimm
June 1st, 2013 Poet from Cornwall, U.K.

Humane Wordsmith

PREMJI IS A NATURAL story teller. He may not have had any formal training in the craft of storytelling, but he excels in narration, in holding the interest of the reader, who is increasingly becoming impatient, due to many distractions in life today. He has a keen eye, minute details of everyday mundane experiences, conversations and reflections on the same create restlessness in him to share his experiences. The reader is amply rewarded, enriched, woken up from inertia, sits up and take notice of life, people, friends, family, co workers, neighbours, events as reported in the media and many other things that make up the delicately woven tapestry of our lives, as this unknown wordsmith, unfolds with simplicity.

Why are we here . . . are we here just to earn out bread and butter, feed our family and egos, or is there a larger purpose? If being born human is the highest gift, then being humane is the ultimate purpose of life. This is the subtle message in his stories. It is apparent that his consciousness doesn't allow him to rest, he is outraged by human apathy, aware of immense possibilities of vitality—invigorating our lives though love, compassion, humour, righteous living.

Almost all the stories are set in Kerala, where he grew up and works. It's a milieu he's familiar with. His style is unique, wittily incisive, tone compassionate. In some ways he reminds one of Ruskin Bond, who's as Indian as Premji in ethos. He weaves affection in his stories for his people like Gerald Durrell does for his characters in his book' My family and other animals'. He makes you wonder if there's any truth in Mark Twain's comment on Indians in—'It is a curious people, with them all life seems to be sacred except human life". One thing is certain his friendly, non judgmental, immensely readable narration will arouse in the reader a curiosity to meet the author and get to know him over several cups of coffee. Simply because there's as much of Premji in the stories as the multitude of lives he captures in his stories.

Nothing escapes his antennas; he is wired 24/7 to life as it unfolds, perhaps in his sleep and dreams too. Such is his engagement with life, his empathy and world view. He writes fearlessly, in a style that is free of any artifice, goes to the heart of the matter, in a simple language, rich in life like images. He is in no hurry to blurt it out. He must have been a fisherman in one of his past births; such is natural flair for throwing bait, hooking the readers' interest. One is amply rewarded. And he knows it! Why be apologetic about the gifts God has blessed you with, he seems to ask tongue in cheek.

While reading the stories, one gets goose pumps, eyes brim with tears, lips relax into a smile, head goes into a spin, chill crawls over the spine, legs become motionless, fingers begin to tremble, heart aches—all in a span of may be 10 minutes depending on your speed and involvement in the stories. The conversational style draws us into his world instantly. He sprinkles one line poems, wisdom that comes with living in awareness, witty one-liners. There is nothing prosaic about his short stories.

If one steps into Premji's world of short fiction, one is likely to come face to face with characters one can relate to, his characters are not flat, dialogue not insipid. He shows remarkable skill in handling the full complexities of the outside and the inner world in a few paragraphs. It won't be an exaggeration that his canvas is as large as that of a novelist—a canvas that unfolds not only the subjective drives, anxieties, frailties, compulsions of an individual, but also the broader issues like environment, social prejudices, erosion of human values, break down of nuclear families. His deep anguish spills over, on helplessly watching that all the safety valves that the community used to have for nourishing the spirit which provided secure and safe environment so integral for living in harmony with nature, others and self have died an unnatural death.

What makes him stand out as an excellent story teller is that he has something vital to share; he has the gift of telling it. Above all, each story revolves around a few characters, one of whom is Premji himself. He takes up one idea, and it is dealt with absolute singleness of aim and directness of method. It is this essential kind of unity which will be found to characterize every really good story ever told d in literature all over the world. Singleness of aim and singleness of effect are, therefore, the two great canons by which we have to try the value of a short story as an art. His stories have rounded characterization, pulsating atmosphere, and interesting elements of surprise, twists and turns. If you have come this far with me, it's obvious you are interested in what an unknown wordsmith wishes to share with you.

To give you a brief preview, a line from his first story—*For your eyes only*

'When you are in love, the whole world shrinks into two pairs of eyes . . .'

Another titled—*Mother of all sorrows*

'Poor woman has nothing to change also and the rich are selling their old clothes at retail chains like Big Bazaar! Bastards'

Next—*Stardust*

'Two months back we were celebrating her birthday. Her two sons joined from US through Skype'.

He makes a comment in the course of the narrative, or makes a character his spokes person. He is like a skilled marksman, hits where it's supposed to hurt. His words pierce the somnolent psyche.

I Hope you'll enjoy these stories as much as I have. Happy Reading

From the desk of Ms Mamta Agarwal, poet and freelance journalist from New-Delhi

1

For Your Eyes Only!

'Surumi turned eighteen today,' the care-taker of that poor home told herself while closing her old diary, which contained every detail of the inmates there. The old woman tried to recollect her innocent face, deep buried in memories . . . the cute little angelic face of an infant girl . . . with dark eyebrows, carefully drawn with the worn out stub of an eyebrow pencil . . . might be the last artwork of a helpless mother on life's canvas, that too before abandoning her fruit of passion! And that's why she kept her name as 'Surumi'.

The financial back up of that poor home was getting deteriorated every day and the caretaker thought of finding a suitable job for her. And at last she succeeded in her endeavor and Surumi was appointed as a sales girl in a huge shopping mall, owned by a wonderful lady who admired the caretaker even from her younger days.

Surumi had to work from morning nine to evening six'o clock and instantly she fell in love with the fresh smell of expensive clothes. The caretaker was quite happy as the Mall owner provided 'pick and drop' facilities for their lady staff. After the evening prayers, Surumi used to tell every day's funny happenings, that too in detail, to her care-taker with childlike innocence.

Later, Surumi was shifted to Children's section as small kids liked her charm very much. 'Beauty with innocence'—that was her plus point according the experienced floor manager. Gradually, Surumi stopped sharing funny stories with the caretaker. She was bit worried at first and her experienced eyes caught Surumi ready-handed, saying 'bye' to the pick and drop cab driver through her beautiful eyes. The old woman was a bit worried, but she didn't say anything. Within a week, one her well-wishers informed her that he had seen Surumi with a blond guy in a nearby Theater. That day she returned back in in the evening by an auto-rickshaw.

'What happened to your pick and drop cab?' the caretaker asked.

'One of its tyres got punctured in the middle . . . Madam,' Surumi replied so innocently.

'And how was the movie? Is that a love story?'

'Movie? I don't understand what you really mean!'

'I was also there . . . Now, do you have anything more to say?'

'Madam . . . I am so sorry . . . Sooraj is in love with me . . . He promised to marry me at the end of this year,' Surumi apologized painfully.

'If he won't?'

'No Madam . . . he won't betray me.'

'If 'not' . . . well and good . . . Falling in love with someone is not at all a sin . . . dear kid . . . I know, you had to live all these days in short of love . . . And naturally you crave for love . . . When you are in love, the whole world shrinks into two pair of eyes . . . Am I correct?'

'You are right . . . Madam'

'Just look into his eyes for some time, tomorrow,' the care taker told calmly while returning to her other duties. 'Orphans are so dear to God . . . But, creating orphans knowingly, is the deadliest of all sins,' she told herself with unending pain.

♥

I was standing on the ground floor, busy negotiating the prices of uniforms with the floor manager for my little boys. School opening is a nightmare for every poor parent!

Surumi was the last one who got out of the cab on the very next day. She went inside and pressed her index finger on the punching machine.

'Excuse me, Madam . . . I forgot to take my purse from the cab . . . May I?' she pleaded for permission from the floor manager.

'O.K . . . But, return fast . . . See . . . customers are there.'

Surumi walked away like a mild breeze . . .

'She is our finest sales girl . . . Mr. Premji,' said the floor manager.

Sooraj was standing near the cab, smoking a cigarette, when she approached.

'Smoking is injurious to health,' Surumi spelled out her protest.

'I will stop it on the very day of our marriage,' he promised while looking into her eyes. 'Surumi . . . You look so beautiful today!'

'Sooraj . . . Will you love me all life?' she kept on looking, so deep into his eyes, though she was blushing to the core . . .

♥

'Are his eyes so beautiful?' the caretaker asked calmly, immediately after the evening prayers.

'Yes Madam,' Surumi replied.

'How long could he maintain eye contact with you?'

'Just . . . a couple of seconds . . .'

'Just a couple of seconds?' she stopped a second . . . 'And what did you see in his eyes?'

'Lust . . . pure lust!' her eyes couldn't hide self-contempt . . . 'Only true lovers can maintain eye-contact for long.'

'Eyes never lie . . . my kid!'

The old woman embraced her with the strength of her strengths! Sometimes, a touch is more powerful than millions of words!

December 07, 2011

2

The Mother Of All Sorrows

THIRTEEN YEAR BACK . . . I was working as a sales engineer, destined to sell huge excavators for a living. The meager income status forced me to share a room with Arun, my best pal, at Elsa tourist home—a nearly dilapidated structure that stood on steel concrete, next to the Trivandrum Medical College. He was a house-surgeon, undergoing one year training period after the completion of MBBS degree (Bachelor of Medicine and Bachelor of Surgery).

Life-saver and a gravedigger! What a grave combination!

'Excessive workload, without proper remuneration and recognition and the notorious hostile approach by authorities and public!' Being a house-surgeon is the toughest period in the life of every medical student. And without their share, it's impossible to run a Medical College!

♥

For the last ten days, Arun was in charge of night duty at the children's ward and literally he was fed up of the noise there . . . never-ending screams of children and women! Usually, he used to return by around seven in the morning and immediately he goes to bed even before brushing his teeth! But, on that day . . . he was sitting awake on bed, keeping a pillow on his lap, with empty eyes.

'Arun, are you not sleeping today?'

'I don't think that I can sleep today,' he sank into the bed and started staring at the ceiling.

'You look very depressed . . . What happened dear friend? Did you have a fight with her?'

'Premji . . . yesterday night, I had to witness the saddest event of my life,' he closed his eyes for some time.

'It was around eight'o clock in the evening and I was sitting in the casualty, all alone, after the completion of rounds. You know, Anitha, my friend, was on leave and luckily there were no serious cases to be taken care of. Then, she came . . . empty-handed . . . with a boy around six years . . . At the very first look, I could understand that he was suffering from Japan fever . . . quite common now in places very near to seashores . . . Poor boy . . . he was shivering with high temperature . . . the fever . . . it had affected his brain,' Arun became silent for a moment.

'Then?' I asked with painful anxiety.

'I admitted him immediately to the intensive care unit (ICU) and started medication after contacting Prof. Dr. Haridas. You know Premji . . . after all it is a government institution . . . we have limitations everywhere . . . Luckily, he started responding to the medicines . . . temperature reduced . . . She was sitting outside the ICU praying silently, while the boy was sleeping inside like uprooted spinach.'

'Did you have anything?' I asked.

'No doctor . . . How is my son? Will he be alright?' she asked.

'Let's hope so,' I consoled her and I summoned one of the attenders to get her some food.

'Sir . . . he is my one and only kid . . . His father is no more and I have no relatives other than him . . . Sir, I was working as a home-nurse in the home of an aged couple . . . My son got this fever from the local school where water is so contaminated . . . They helped me get some medical aid from a nearby private hospital . . . but, how can a helpless mother like me meet the expenses,' poor woman, aged around thirty seven, wiped her tears with her very old faded cotton Sari like her faded life.

Poor woman didn't have anything to change also and the rich are selling their old clothes at retail chains like Big Bazaar! Bastards! I felt a twinge of pain deep within.

'Don't worry . . . He will be alright by His mercy,' I tried to console her before going back to casualty.

Another mother with a very beautiful young girl appeared in the casualty. She was also admitted to the ICU. Both the women sat on long chairs, outside ICU.

♥

It was nearing eleven thirty and I checked the boy's condition again. But, his condition was getting deteriorated fast. 'Anything might happen,' the empty face of the aged nurse stood beside me warned. She might have seen thousands of cases like this in her service life! I should inform her as early as possible.

How to break a bad news? It's really important for any Doctor as there are maximum possibilities of getting hit! She was waiting for me near the ICU entrance, and the other woman was sleeping on dirty floor, covered with mosquitoes.

'Sir, how is he?' she asked while looking into my eyes.

Eyes, they are the most dangerous organs in human body as they cannot hide lies!

'He is not,' I tried to tell the truth, but she didn't allow me to complete.

'Sir . . . please, save my son . . . I have nobody other than him . . . Sir, this moment . . . you are my God . . . you are God . . . you can save him . . . Sir . . . you can only save him . . . you are my God,' poor woman was so confident in a doctor like me!

'God! Where are you! And where am I?' My heart started screaming for his mercy . . .

I went back and tried to sleep little bit, sitting on my chair. You can sleep in war-torn Somalia peacefully . . . but, it is quite unthinkable in any cities in Kerala! Mosquitoes fly around like continuous bullet fire from enemy guns . . . Garbage . . . Garbage everywhere . . . Even an IAS officer's wife throws garbage straight on the road! God! Please give me some chloroform . . . let me sleep for some time!

♥

'Sir, please come with me . . . the boy started gasping,' the aged nurse woke me up at around two'o clock and I followed her to the ICU.

'Let's give him Oxygen,' I said. 'The ventilator is out of order.'

'Sir . . . I don't think he will.'

'No assumptions . . . let's pray,' I couldn't take away my eyes from his cherubic face.

Sadly I knew . . . she was right . . . She had witnessed many more deaths than me!

'Sir, let's inform her . . . otherwise it's going to be a problem.'

There she was on the dead cold dirty floor.

'Let her sleep,' I didn't want to interrupt her last peaceful slumber.

'As you wish,' the nurse went back.

♥

'Sir . . . he is no more,' the nurse informed me at around four'o clock in the morning.

We woke her up.

'Sir . . . my son?' she asked in panic.

'Dear sister . . . See . . . I am no God . . . I am just a helpless Doctor,' I couldn't speak any further. Something was chocking my soul . . .

'Sir?' She stood like struck by a lightening.

'Yes . . . he is no more,' the experienced nurse informed her calmly.

She sat on the chair, closing her face with her empty hands and we stood beside her like two stone pillars. She lifted up her head after five minutes.

'Sir, will you please do me a favour?' She asked calmly.

'Yes . . . surely . . . please tell me.'

'Sir . . . Please make immediate arrangements . . . that young girl in ICU will lose her eyesight . . . if the corneas in both of her eyes are not replaced within a week . . . how sad . . . Let her see the world through his eyes.'

'And then?' I couldn't resist my heart.

'She walked away in the darkness' replied Dr. Arun . . . 'Empathy, thy name is mother!'

January 19, 2012

3

Stardust

'Premjeeee,' my wife began to shout from the kitchen.

'Please don't eat my brains in the morning . . . dear . . . You know, I am writing a story.'

'You can keep on writing stories to astonish your readers! But, don't forget that 'you' have two small boys . . . If you don't take care of them right now, leave them forever,' she couldn't control her anger. (Yes . . . she is right . . . Most artists never care their families! An unfortunate universal truth!)

'Dad, get us Flintstones,' my younger son started shouting.

'Idiot . . . who are you to command me? See . . . I am your Dad . . . Add 'please' before that 'get'. Understand?' I poured the same anger upon him.

'Yes Dad.'

'O.K . . . What's that?'

'A cartoon DVD . . . Gloria Aunt has a copy.'

'Anger is a dirty form of energy, which will retrace the origin. Don't you know that?' my elder son asked.

'What?'

'You only taught us!'

'Is that so?'

♥

Gloria aunt, an Anglo-Indian woman, is living all alone in a beautiful heritage home in Fort-Cochin. Arabian Sea is at a stone-throw distance from her home. Her father, a heavily paid employee of Kolar Gold Mines, purchased that beautiful building way back in the forties. Her twin-sons Wilfred and Alfred, now residing in US, force her to join them almost every day. But, she never cares!

Being her next-door neighbor, I have a very special place in her heart. Sometimes, she calls me either 'Alfred' or 'Wilfred' and I call her 'Mamma'. She loves me a lot since I am an ardent listener of her well-crafted stories. I love her a lot since she has the biggest collection of movies: DVD's of classics from almost every language on earth to local disasters! Whenever Alfred or Wilfred visits her, they bring an aircraft full of movies and she keeps them in a very orderly manner. But, now-a-days, she prefers cartoons and I am afraid, my sons would replace me soon from her heart!

'Everybody will become a child in the fag-end of their lives!' she laughed.

♥

Two months back . . .

We were celebrating her seventieth birthday. Her sons too joined from US through 'skype.' Internet kills distance and time too! That's why every Airline company across the world is sinking! If they come to know about this fact, sure they would contact some criminal gangs to cut those thick Internet cables laid under the sea, connecting continents! World is just a small playground now! Tomorrow, it's going to be the biggest jail!

Some rare DVDs of 'Shyam,' a local 'heavy-head-weight champion' superstar, was my birthday present to her since he was her favorite local actor.

'Premji . . . Shyam is a terrific actor . . . I have decided to give him a treat someday . . . I love his dreamy . . . romantic . . . eyes . . . real 'Stardust!"

'Mamma . . . One day . . . Sure, I will try to bring him here as a surprise . . . Together, you both can enact an old love song.'

'You naughty,' Mamma got angry.

Woman looks so beautiful when she is angry! Try to make her laugh then! If possible, she will never leave you!

♥

Shyam, the aging superstar, was traveling in his brand new BMW 7 series car, the latest addition to his fleet. The soothing music, that too from one of his blockbusters, dissolved into the ears of his driver.

He tried to cover the wrinkles around his neck by a colorful muffler. Repeated injections of Botox, made his facial wrinkles improved. If the effect of that muscle relaxant could last for two years at least, he wished sincerely. He cursed the poor quality make-up materials of yesteryears, which added infinite amount of toxins to his body, silently.

'Maintaining one's own popularity is a real burden,' he touched his arc-light-tanned hands. 'It could disfigure me some day,' he told himself while closing the expensive mirror fixed behind the front seat.

'Sam, pull over the car that side.'

He jumped out immediately after the car made an abrupt stop and started walking swiftly toward that heritage home adjacent to the sea. His aged knees, not ready to agree with his stardom, had begun to pain. What to do? The show must go on!

♥

'Crazy idiot,' Sam thought while standing beside the luxury car. Poor man desperately wanted to become an actor. He even changed him name to 'Sam', a word having close resemblance to 'Shyam'. But, unfortunately he could only get transformed to a 'driver with star value!'.

'Someday, he will give me also a chance,' it was the most repeated dialogue in his life.

'Get lost,' he started pelting stones at the crows resting peacefully on the branches of trees near-by.

'Single dropping on his car . . . lousy bastard will make me eat that,' he told himself. 'Every Car dealer gives him cars almost half the rate as a reward for 'hidden reference' and he gets enough margin when he sells it off with a new branding: 'a car used by Shyam'

A very beautiful teenage girl passed by.

'O! This is Shyam Sir's car,' a lovely sentence escaped from her beautiful mouth. 'Will you please introduce me to him?' she asked innocently.

'Sure . . . but,' Sam stopped in the middle.

'But?'

'What is my benefit?' His eyes started crawling down through her well-shaped body.

'Get lost . . . you . . . ,' she walked away and the crows started making horrible noise as if they were congratulating her!

♥

'Shyam,' Gloria Aunt couldn't believe her eyes. 'Premji is a wonderful guy . . . He kept his promise'

'Who is Premji?'

'My next door neighbor and a writer himself . . . He promised me to bring you here!'

'I am afraid; I do not know any Premji. I just dropped in . . . That's all,' he smiled

'Please take your seat,' Gloria Aunt requested him while searching for the remote control to switch off the T.V. The movie, running, was one of his blockbusters of yesteryears!

'No need to switch that off . . . Just reduce the volume a little,' the Narcissus in him told. He was desperately in need of another super-hit like that to survive in the most unstable industry ever: 'The Cinema'. A causeless uneasiness started creeping through his soul.

'O.K . . . Let me get you some chilled French Wine?'

'That will be a wonderful choice!'

'By that time, if you want, you can freshen up there,' Aunt showed her expensive toilet.

Shyam left happily, that too after thirty minutes long conversation with 'the fan of his life'!

'Mamma, you could have called me,' I couldn't hide my disappointment.

'Sorry Premji . . . You know . . . at that time . . . I thought . . . that . . . I was in cloud-nine,' Mamma replied innocently.

'O.K . . . Then . . . what did he talk with you? I like the authentic way, he talks to the media . . . Please . . . tell in detail'

'O . . . there was nothing important,' she told, uninterested.

'Mamma . . . you disappoint me.'

'He is not 'Stardust,' my son, as I thought earlier.'

'Then?'

'Bloody star-waste!'

It was the first time in my life; I heard a rough word from her mouth.

'Mammaaa.'

'Yes . . . Mamma only . . . Do you know, what did he say . . . immediately after handing over this visiting card, before he had left?'

'No.'

'If I am ready to sell this house, anytime, I am free enough to contact him! Real estate is his main business . . . it seems . . . and he would give me the best offer . . . Cunning bastards, who debaucherize art, are roaming in expensive cars to befool poor people . . . Premji . . . You . . . You should write this for the sake of me,' Mamma commanded like Queen Victoria!

May 24, 2012

4

Christmas Greetings

Christmas was only two weeks away. And I was wandering through the newly opened shopping mall in the city, to purchase some inexpensive gifts for friends and relatives, along with my younger son.

'Dad, please get me also a greeting card . . . for a very special friend of mine,' my seven year old lad demanded coolly.

Christmas is a nightmare for parents, poor, like me.

'Very special friend? Is it for your girlfriend?'

'Daaaaaaaaaad,' poor boy was getting angry.

'Sorry young-man . . . I was just kidding you,' I tried to calm him down. 'O.K . . . Do you want an expensive card or so?'

'No . . . He doesn't like expensive things . . . I need a simple one,' he stopped in the middle.

'But, elegant?'

'Yes'

Christmas was over and so the holidays. Continuous ringing bicycle bells, woke me up from deep slumber at around four'o clock, in the evening.

'Unfortunately, the postal department couldn't locate the addressee,' postman told while returning the greeting card. 'We are extremely sorry,' the old man pedaled away with a naughty smile on his pale face.

Tears blinded my eyes, while going through the unfamiliar 'To address'.

JESUS

VATICAN

November 26, 2012

5

Storks Of Sumeko

It was a bright evening in the spring. Soumya was standing near the front gate of her palatial house, awaiting the school bus.

'My daughter is getting skinnier everyday . . . She is so tired after the school . . . poor kid,' anxious thoughts kept on gushing out through her mind as her six year old daughter Shruthi was the fruit of thirteen years of infertility treatment. Whatever food, that too made after a lot of research from noted cookery books, remained almost untouched every evening! Why evenings . . . everyday! She wished to plant bombs on every torturing cell named schools! Stupid society! And their silly education!

'Hi . . . Premji,' Soumya waved her hands when I was about to cross her by bike.

'Hi . . . Saumya'

I stopped the bike, a little ahead of her, by jamming the breaks. It creaked a lot before coming into halt!

'When are you going to throw away this junk?' she teased me:

You are nothing but a friend in front of a childhood friend!

'Not in the near future!' I laughed. 'Then . . . how is life?'

'Same routine . . . getting her ready for school in the morning . . . household duties . . . that will be over by ten . . . the watching 'the never ending serials in T.V . . . You know . . . the heroin of the best running serial didn't deliver even after two years of pregnancy!'

'Idiotic! Is she an elephant?'

'May be,' she laughed aloud. 'And waiting for Shruthi in the evening and then teaching her . . . preparing her project works'

'The same routine of a 'Gulf widow',' I teased her.

'You know . . . Premji . . . For just two kilometers, they take her around ten kilometers everyday . . . every school bus operates like that . . . they have to drop other kids too at their doorsteps'

'Just two kilometers . . . and your car is lying idle . . . Why can't you drop her every day?'

'First of all . . . I don't know how to drive! I am really scared, when I see a vehicle approaching from the other side! And who knows . . . what will be left with when you return back! Thieves move around, more free than Policemen, that too in broad daylight!' she laughed again.

'Idiot! A wonderful woman like you should never depend on others . . . Just one week is enough! I will make arrangements for that.'

'Thank you . . . I will try my level best.'

'When is your husband coming back from Dubai?'

'By next week . . . don't worry, Premji . . . your quota will be taken cared of . . . What's that? Aaah . . . Bacardi . . . ,' she smiled. 'Recession has nothing to do with alcohol!'

'Thank you.'

'Premji . . . why are you crazy of that bitter stuff?'

'First it tastes bitter . . . then better.'

We laughed.

♥

Shruthi used to sit beside Akhila in the school bus everyday as she was her guardian angel. Akhila, studying in seventh standard, is a voracious reader and that day she was reading the translation of a Japanese book taken from school library, telling the story of Sumeko.

'Chechee . . . (Elder sister) . . . Please, tell me also the story,' Shruthi requested as she was fascinated by the colorful illustrations.

'Molu . . . This is the story of a young Japanese girl named Sumeko . . . She was the victim of Atom bombs, dropped in Japan during Second World War . . . understand,' Akhila started a new story as daily routine.

'Yes'

'Do you know what a war is?'

'Yes . . . lots of people die . . . I have seen it on T.V.'

'O.K . . . some sixty five years back . . . Americans dropped two atoms bombs in Japan . . . one in Hiroshima and other in Nagasaki . . . three hundred thousand people dead . . . How many people were dead?'

'Three hundred,' Shruthi stopped in the middle.

'Thousand . . . O.K . . . and another three hundred thousand people were affected by its radiation'

'Chechee . . . what is meant by radiation?'

'What is radiation? How to explain her?' Akhila was bit confused. 'Ah . . . it's heat . . . the heat of the bomb blast . . . And Sumeko was a small girl like her,' she pointed at ten year old beautiful girl with Rosy cheeks, sitting on the other row of seats. 'Our . . . poor . . . Sumeko was also exposed to that heat . . . You know . . . the heat of Atom bomb can cause blood cancer.'

'There is no cure for it . . . isn't it Chechee? Mummy was telling that the other day to our next door aunt,' Shruthi shared some information innocently.

'Yes . . . You are right . . . In Japanese, they call the radiation victims like her as 'Hibakusha' . . . And Sumeko was diagnosed suffering from blood cancer . . . She was getting weaker and weaker everyday . . . One day, someone told her a simple cure,'

'What was that?'

'Making paper storks . . . Make a thousand paper storks . . . Then death will step away.'

'That's interesting,' Shruthi said.

'She started making them and her condition was getting better . . . But, she couldn't complete a thousand,' Akhila gave proper modulation to her voice as a trained dubbing artist.

'Did Sumeko die?'

'Yes . . . when she died, her friends counted the paper storks . . . there were six hundred storks, of different colours, in her collection. How many?'

'Six hundred . . . a very sad story Chechee . . . today I will tell it to Mummy,' Shruthi told painfully while going through the sketches in that well illustrated book. The last page contained a line diagram . . . how to make a paper stork . . .

♥

'Please make me one,' Shruthi started pleading her. 'pleeeease.'

'No . . . No . . . Not now,' Akhila was not interested.

'Pleeeeeease . . . Checheeee,'

Akhila couldn't resist the innocence in her and she tore a sheet of white paper from her notebook. The bus was running at average speed and she completed the paper stork as per instructions. And at last she made a beak just by folding on end.

'It's so beautiful,' Shruthi gave a surprise kiss to Akhila.

Happily, Akhila went back to the book.

'War is evil,' Shruthi played with its lovely wings throughout the journey. 'War is evil . . . otherwise Sumeco wouldn't have died'

♥

The school bus stopped at her stop.

'Bye . . . Chechee . . . ,' Shruthi was ready to jump out of the bus . . . from the cage of letters to the comfort of her freedom zone named home . . .

School bags were heaped at one corner of the bus and Saumya collected her heavy school bag from the Ayah, caretaker woman. The bus driver, an old-man, was waiting for the Ayah to close the door.

Suddenly, the stork had a strange wish: to fly up in the strong west wind, as it had fallen down from the hands of Shruthi. Ayah closed the door and the bus was about to move slowly as he gradually released the clutch pedal.

'You can't escape from me . . . ,' Shruthi managed to catch hold of the paper stork's tail.

Quickly, the white paper stork turned blood-Red . . .

December 30, 2011

6

Woman Of Substance

Even though it is district headquarters, Mandya is not a big city like Mysore (The Garden City of India). I had to spend four years there, to complete engineering degree. Four years . . . God! What all I had seen . . . from agitations of farmers caused by narrow minded politicians . . . to bloodbaths by fanatics immediately after the demolition of Babri Mazjid . . . every form of human madness . . . I am destined to bear all those in my soul.

Our hostel was just a stone throw away from the heart of the city. Sharing of 'Kauvery' river water was a burning issue between two states, Karnataka and Tamilnadu. As a result, Mandya City was under curfew. Farmers of Mandya were not ready to give water for the agriculturists of Tamilnadu. Why future wars . . . water causes for bloodshed every day!

'Why should a river flow through two states?' a madcap started singing.

'Just to make another river of blood!' his blind companion also joined the song with deep melancholy.

Agitating farmers were about to burn a petrol bunk, immediately opposite to our hostel, in the evening. Tear gas shells were fired and unfortunately they landed on our hostel ground! Students, already trapped in curfew, were trapped again inside the tear gas fumes and that time I was sleeping inside a new blanket. My classmate Vinod had a very tough time as his eyes started swelling. We used to call him 'Bulb' because of his ever-bulged eyes and that time it was exactly the same. Curfew was relaxed after two days and his father reached our hostel. He was a Bangalorean.

'Premji, if I arrange a rented house outside, would you like to share that with Vinod? You know, he is a bit afraid of living alone', Jay uncle, Vinod's father, asked.

'Sure Uncle' . . . Even, I too suffer from low blood caused by poor food supplied in the hostel', I promised him since he was my best pal. 'Snoopy will also join us.'.

Jay uncle became very happy.

♥

'If you vacate the hostel, be ready to face the consequences. If you Dad comes to know about this . . . that's all . . . there ends your engineering', mother warned me when I rang up and told her the matter.

Who cares the threats of Moms! That too at the noon of your youth! Even I needed a change . . . It was a wonderful new house in the outskirts of the city and we were the first tenants. There was a huge ground behind our housing colony and children used to play Cricket there. Soon, Jayaram Reddy also joined us. I was forced to learn the alphabets of cooking from our cook Maheswari. Whenever there might be a festival or something, she would be missing! Days went by happily and freshers joined our college. The tough times of ragging started, but we used to do only friendly ragging! It was fun for them as well as for us!

Just opposite of our house, lived a bank employee and his family. His two small daughters were my best friends. Local boy Krishna used to help us bringing vegetables, grinding rice for breakfast and transferring silly gossips. Months passed . . . One day, I was busy watching Sudha, a wonderful girl of sixteen, riding slowly on her bicycle. She just smiled and sped away.

'Premji Sir, there is no point in watching her,'local boy Krishna said from behind.

'When did you come?'I was angry.

'Just now.'

'Why did you say so?'

'She is dumb, Sir.'

'What?'

'She cannot talk . . . she can only hear.'

'So what? Thanks God!' I said aloud

'Thank God!' poor Krishna was embarrassed . . .

♥

Automobile Engineering was quite a dry branch and girls from other branches used to care only very handsome guys. I was an alien among them . . . with a French beard! (What could I do if my beard had been growing just like that and that time it was not all a part of fashion!).

Nobody had any interest on Sudha. The finest language ever in the history of mankind is silence and of course that is the language of love! And we were enjoying that silence . . . Sudha . . . O! The nectar of love! Semester vacations started . . . Sudha, where are you, little darling?

We all returned soon as semester breaks were so short and unfortunately I was the class topper! It was quite unexpected! Everyone started teasing me . . . topper . . . topper . . . Idiots, I was a lazy guy during the past three years and now you see my real potential, I thought . . . But, I had to suffer a lot for that! That's another story.

'Now, submit your synopsis for project work', Mr. Naganna, our HOD, announced in the class room. He was a diehard 'Stalinist' professor! Shridhar and I . . . we both looked at each other . . .

'Old man is going to fuck someone's happiness!' he told in a lower tone.

Discussions were going on everywhere to find out a new concept to convince the HOD. I was busy converting that as an opportunity to grab some more money from my Dad! Naturally discussions steamed up even in our rented house, till night. At around 10'O clock, our fiends left for hostel and I locked the front gate. Being a very cold night of February, everyone slept off early in the nearby houses . . . everyone finished eating dinner except me. When I was about to start eating, calling bell started ringing continuously.

'Bastards jumped over the gate,' Snoopy said.

'Hostel gate might have been closed. Let them sleep here. Reddy, Open the door', Vinod said.

He went to open the front door. But, someone pushed him inside swiftly. Just sheer luck, he didn't fall down.

'Hey . . . what the fuck is going on?' I shouted?

'We have taken over this house', a six and half feet tall body builder answered. 'Shut your arse and keep quiet tonight . . . otherwise', he demonstrated the punch of a boxer.

I knew this guy, henchman of a local MLA (Member of legislative assembly). He grabbed the gate key and switched off all the lights. Suddenly a gang of four members moved into our house with some plastic bags. They all sat on the dining hall floor in semi-darkness. The Moon was rising up, quite late . . .

'Hoy . . . Give some glasses and water,' the muzzle man asked

They started boozing and we were standing in the front room. They could see us . . . Fear . . . nothing but fear, we were! We stood there as if observing silence.

'Boss, did you have dinner?' one of the gang members asked the muzzle man. That was a familiar voice.

'No . . . Mahesha,' Boss replied. 'I didn't get time . . . You know . . . I was searching for a safe house where students live.'

'Then, have it'. Mahesha handed over my plate of chapattis and curry.

Boss grabbed the plate and started eating like a hungry lion.

'Bastard! Who will water the fire in my belly?' I thought in vain . . .

Suddenly a bike stopped just outside our house. A tall guy and someone in a huge jacket entered into our rented house.

'God! She is a whore', Snoopy said in a low voice, 'that guy was our senior in college'

'Welcome . . . Welcome . . . 'Mysorina Malligai . . . (The Jasmine of Mysore)', Boss welcomed her pleasantly.

'O . . . I am flattered', she replied in sexy voice.

I could feel the feeble smell of some Jasmines on her plaited hair. Suddenly the smell of drunken lust started mixing with that of Jasmine.

'Boys, switch on the front room light and continue your studies', Boss ordered. 'And you guys, just keep quiet', he ordered to his gang.

Again the cloud of fear started moving across our mind-skies.

'Enjoy yourself Boss', Mahesha said with happiness. Boss vanished with her and the cot made of some cheap wood started creaking.

'Vinod, your bed is gone!', I said. Poor guy couldn't even smile.

Vinod, Snoopy and Jayaram were lying on a bed sheet spread on the floor and I was sitting on its corner. We didn't talk even a single word. What an insult! But, to my surprise, they all slept off coolly as if nothing had happened! The bedroom door used to open and close, loads of lusts were transferred. I heard her snoring in the middle! 'Quenching of lust', still continued! Then Mahesha came to my room in a jolly mood. He was working as a supplier in the Hostel.

'Mahesha, what is this? How come, you are with this gang?'

'Boss called me . . . So I am here. Forget it all, Premji . . . now, go and enjoy her. This is the best chance to lose your virginity', Mahesh teased me.

'Fuck you. Now, leave me alone'. I couldn't even think of surrendering my treasure to that bitch! I switched of the light and sat there like a metal statue. Police party might appear for night patrolling. The Moon was getting deep buried in darkness of clouds . . . and I . . . in deep insult . . .

'Three times, in just three hours . . . Boss, you have great stamina,' another guy praised the Boss

They all slept off and time passed on snail pace. I had to wake them at 5'O clock in the morning. Better, they could have killed me! And at last the wall clock told me . . . 'boy . . . it's time to wake them up'. The Boss wanted to have it once again. But, his mates didn't allow that. She was sleeping peacefully in the bed. Boss woke her up from deep slumber . . . 'Get up . . . bitch'

'Come, let's go now'

'Now?'

'Yes, now,' the sound of Boss started rising. 'Almost everyone knows us here'

'Do you have a vehicle?'she asked in a sleepy voice.

'Yes'

'Mysorina Malligai.' She was ready for another act in real life. My God! From where had she picked up those Jasmines? Some among the gang vanished in the dark and Mahesh rolled out the bike. Boss had a plan to leave her in the Bus stand. She moved out slowly and the Boss followed. My friends were snoring like old dogs in the other room. 'House is burning and idiots are sleeping . . . bastards' I too followed them, just to close the door.

'Sorry Boss,' Boss told me . . . 'Hotel rooms are not safe now-a-days. If you have any problem in Mandya, just tell to Mahesha. I will manage it'

What an offer from a gangster!

They crossed the gate and Boss closed it without any noise. Mahesha started the bike and he was in a hurry to transport her away.

'I will not go by this bike,' she was reluctant to sit on it.

'Don't talk . . . just go by this bike,' Boss caught hold of her hair in anger.

Somehow, she managed to release her hair from his grab and ran towards the ground in darkness. Boss followed her and tried to pull her back to the bike . . . But, she started shouting bad words . . . Might be out of fear . . . Boss kicked on her lower abdomen, so merciless he was, that the entire housing colony woke up of her screams . . . Luckily, she didn't faint . . .

'Shit,' the Boss ran towards the bike and they vanished in the dark.

'Bastards . . . Sons of bitches,' she continued shouting while writhing in pain. My friends woke up.

'What happened?' Vinod asked.

'Can't you see?'I was mad with anger and hunger. Bastards slept off very well and now asking: what happened! He she kept on cursing and local people started gathering. They were looking us with contempt . . . God!

'Sons of whores . . . who drank my blood the whole night . . . how can he kick me so brutally? I just asked for a single favour . . . It is not safe even for a prostitute to sit alone in that Bus stand. Every male is a sex maniac . . . Bastards . . . Bastards,'she kept on shouting in pain.

At last, it was 6'O clock in the morning and slanting rays of morning Sun fell on her face. She was around forty and her face was yellow in colour . . . Turmeric paste? Of course, she had to heal the scratches on her face . . . Her life was eaten away by Vultures!

Then our cook Maheswari appeared for making breakfast. Somehow, she came to know everything.

'These boys are innocent . . . You also know that . . . Now, leave this place . . . Those guys are gangsters . . . They used to do this in other houses too where students are staying alone . . . see, they may want to kill you if you don't leave,' Maheswary threatened her.

'Let them kill me,' she sat on our door step.

The people who had gathered dissolved for their daily routine and Maheswari went to the kitchen. The other woman didn't even move from the steps. She sat on the white tiles. Red Sari and white tiles . . . what a contrast!

We were not in a position to explain what happened. At last Vinod asked her to leave raising his voice. Snoopy and Reddy joined with him.

'It's not our fault,' they tried to explain.

'It's your fault only . . . then, why did you open the door? You are also a part of this game,' she shouted while pressing her abdomen. 'If I tell the Police that you all had enjoyed me . . . then imagine what will happen . . .'

♥

Sudha stopped her bicycle in front of our house and our eyes met. I could see the clouds of contempt even on her face. She sped away in disgust. Malligai was watching that . . . Can she understand my plight?

'God! I lost everything . . . food, sleep, honour and at last love! Sudha, please . . . please don't misunderstand me,' unknown feeling were doing 'thandava' (cosmic dance) in my mind. My friends, everyone, failed to plead her. Sadness started flooding on their faces. They looked at my face . . . Were there a silent request? Premji, do something . . .

Her eyes resembled that of a stuffed animal.

♥

'Akkaa' (elder sister), I started talking with her. She was shocked as if touched by a hot metal. 'You know the truth . . . that we are innocent . . . last night, we were totally helpless . . . Akkaa, Vinod is a patient and that's why we took this house for rent . . . Now, we have to leave this place also . . . I know . . . you can understand our plight . . . Akkaa, Please leave . . . Please don't put us in more perils'.

She looked at my face for some time, all the time her left hand pressing her lower abdomen.

'Akkaa, do you want something to drink?'I asked.

She nodded her head.

I handed over a cup of hot coffee to her and she drank peacefully. We were looking at her face. She avoided my friends purposely.

'Thammaa, (younger brother,' what is your name?'she asked me.

'Premji'

'Prem, Last night . . . I was listening to you, talking with Mahesha.'

'But, you were sleeping.'

'I haven't slept for the past 17 years'. A drop of tear started rolling down through her cheek. 'You had a free chance to have it with a woman . . . but, you denied it straight away. Why? Because, you respect women . . . If the man whom I loved . . . at least showed a bit of that . . . then I wouldn't have been like this,'she started crying and her tear drops fell on the floor which split into millions of tiny droplets . . . I felt, my mind crushed like minced meat . . . She handed over the empty glass to me.

'Prem . . . nanna Thammaa . . . (My brother) . . . I am so sorry . . . don't worry . . . my boy . . . I am leaving.'

'Thanks Akkaa,' my friends thanked her immediately. Bloody opportunists!

She walked away slowly and my friends ran to kitchen . . . to have their share of Coffee . . . At last, she vanished from my vision . . . I felt very thirsty as if I was trapped in a desert for days . . . When I was about to close the front door, I felt like, she was sitting there on the steps.

There was nothing . . . except a pool of blood . . .

God! What should I call her?

July 05, 2011

7

A Christmas Carol

'Premji, I should go home, today afternoon,' my friend Suman informed me over mobile phone, somewhere around eleven'o in the morning.

'What's the matter, Suman?'

'My wife is not feeling well . . . It seems, she has vomiting sensations'

'Is she pregnant?'

'She supposes so,'

'God bless you . . . Suman'

'Thanks . . . Premji . . . I will be back by tomorrow morning.'

♥

Making an urban girl pregnant is not an easy task now-a-days! The pizzas, burgers and all the junk food she eats can easily decay her ovum like pumpkins in a compost pit; where sperms, move around like earth worms, can only accelerate the disintegration! Five years! It's a quite long period!

Suman and I, we share a tiled house in the outskirts of that town. It was nearing seven'o clock in the evening. The chillness of December started her silent torment and it was really boring to go out, all alone, for food. Luckily I could locate some semi-ripe bananas, kept in a container away from hungry rats. I chopped them into small pieces and kept for boiling.

'Boiled bananas will be fantastic with black tea,' I told myself.

The induction cooker started making noise and I switched off the power.

'Shit . . . ,' two or three fire-flies were lying above the water surface, well cooked, along with boiled bananas! 'What to do?'

It was pitch-dark outside and the petrol tank of my Yamaha bike remained empty like the breasts of a hunger-struck Somalian mother! And to add more darkness to the situation, pen torch batteries were also drained out!

'Premji . . . in China, sports-men eat insect fries . . . you know . . . they are protein enriched food!' someone told from the memories.

'Is it?' the literary sportsman in me doubted!

'Yes'

'Here we go . . .,' I threw the fire-flies away. 'nhum . . . bananas, boiled in fire-fly stock, is a variety food during Christmas . . .'

♥

I closed all the doors and settled with my laptop to write another episode of autobiographical fiction. But, I was interrupted by a mobile ring. Poetess Angelina was on the line.

'Hi Angel . . . Happy Christmas in advance'

'O! Hi Premji . . . Thank you . . . Same to you'

'Then?'

'I got in contact with a key person from Mac-Millan publishing company . . . She told me to submit the manuscript named 'Universal call for peace' . . . with an introduction'

'Sounds great!'

'I have selected one poem each, of our poet friends and mailed to her'

'Let's hope for the best . . . None is there to publish poetry now-a-days . . . !'

'So true . . . I will let you know if there is any improvement . . . Bye . . . Premji . . . Good night'

'Bye Angel . . . Good night'

Poetry! The crest jewel of art is left unread and unsold! A deep melancholy started encompassing my soul.

♥

Solitude is the best friend of an artist! I have reserved a bullet for that bastard who told it!

I started reading a PDF book . . . Celestine Prophecy . . . I fell in love is his philosophy and critical mass theory. Again my mobile started ringing.

'Premji, tomorrow is declared as a holiday,' Suman was on the line.

'You are lucky, my friend!'

'Happy Christmas'

'Happy New Year too . . . we won't be meeting again till Jan 2nd.'

'Yes . . . same to you'

'Suman, how is your wife? Is she?'

'No . . . it was due to some shabby junk food,' his voice became pale.

♥

'It's nine'o clock,' the display of the mobile phone informed me. Suddenly, the songs and drum beats of a Carol group fell on my ears, approaching, and its intensity kept on increasing.

Our house was located at the dead end of that narrow lane and fortunately we didn't have any neighbors nearby. The sounds were approaching closer. I then checked my wallet. Fortunately or unfortunately, one and only 'five hundred rupee' was left with.

'This is going to be a problem,' I told myself.

'Christmas Carol is a money making business now-a-days . . . Premji,' our 'local Santa Clause' Lonappan Chettan told me yesterday, while having break-fast at Sam Kutty's restaurant. 'Twenty five years . . . for twenty five years . . . I was the Santa of this small town . . . You see my long white beard . . . It's my commitment to Santa . . . But'

'But?'

'I was kicked out last year . . . when people started paying cash as gifts to Santa!'

'Cash gifts to Santa!'

'Yes . . . to make him also greedy!'

'Really sad'

'I know . . . but . . . ,' Lonappan Chettan stopped for some seconds. 'Premji . . . one should give a chance for the gangsters too . . . to repent!' He started laughing.

♥

'Tomorrow is going to be a holiday . . . Nobody will be there in my office . . . My ATM account is already empty . . . I got an e-mail from them yesterday . . . New generation banks are so cunning! If I give the Carol guys this five hundred rupees note . . . that's all! My entire programs will collapse! How can I go home? From whom I can borrow some money from this city quite new to me?' Millions of thoughts started evolving from my tormented soul! Is there a way out?

Yes!

I switched off all the lights and sat there silently in the darkness. The lights, the drum beats were approaching. I watched them diverting their journey to the cross-lanes through the key hole. Gradually the drum beats nullified and I switched on the room light.

What to do now? Shall I watch a comedy movie?

'Life is beautiful,' that Oscar winning Italian comedy movie failed bitterly to make me laugh.

Jesus, where did I lose my laughter? Jesus, where did I lose my happiness?

It was nearing eleven in the night and the drum beats started approaching again. I stood out, wearing the best clothes of mine, waiting for the jingle bells . . . that five hundred rupees note was there in my shirt pocket, so close to my heart. Why should I worry when you are with me . . . Jesus! Why should I be afraid!

Yes . . . I could see the red cloak and white beard of Santa . . . I could see the gas lights . . . the drums . . . and the tall boys . . . singing and rejoicing . . .

Come . . . come . . . come to my house . . . Let's sing and rejoice . . .

But, they took a sudden turn to other cross-road and walked away.

December 28, 2011

8

Everything Has A Price!

'The toughest task on earth is to manage a child,' my colleague Sheela Thomas declared in the staff room that afternoon.

'I don't think your younger son is a problem kid . . . May be you have to change your hostile approach toward him,' I objected her argument, even-though I knew she was right.

'Premji . . . I bet . . . you can't even spend a single day with him . . . he is so naughty,' she couldn't continue the conversation as some Students Union leaders entered in.

'Sir . . . We need your permission to decorate our college auditorium,' Arun requested me.

'What's the matter?'

'Sir . . . We are planning to release our college magazine tomorrow afternoon . . . Just now only we could confirm our chief guest'

'Who is our chief guest?'

'Subhash . . . The new hero of Malayalam Cinema'

'Who is he?'

'Sir . . . Don't you know him? He is the hero of one recent hit film . . . A remake movie . . . 'Stone-lotus' . . . Superb actor, he is!' The boys kept on praising him while I was unsuccessfully wrestling with my mind to remember his face.

'O.K . . . Will he come for the function tomorrow? We can't completely believe these film actors'

'Sure, Sir . . . he will come . . . His house is here only . . . and he will be coming to take his parents to Kochi, where he stays now,' another boy said.

'So, he is a local boy! That's a wonderful piece of information . . . Anyway, is your magazine ready to distribute among students?'

'Yes Sir . . . We have to release it soon . . . You know . . . students union election date will be announced soon . . . If we can't do that in time, we won't be able to secure enough votes . . . These things are common in student politics'; current lady vice chairman of our college shared her anxiety.

'If that's the case . . . O.K . . . You can proceed'

'Sir, one more thing . . . You will have to deliver the presidential address . . . Our Principal will on leave tomorrow'

They walked away coolly putting me in dare straights!

'The toughest task on earth is to manage our students . . . Tomorrow, you are going to know that,' Sheela Thomas laughed loudly and my other colleagues also joined with her.

'Why do you threaten me like this?'

'Premji . . . You are a fresher to our college . . . You know . . . Not even a single function had been completed without a clash between students so far . . . And one more funny thing, they didn't print even a single copy at all!'

'How do you know that?'

'I am the magazine advisor!' She laughed again. 'Tomorrow, they are going to release a fake magazine with white paper inside a Magazine cover . . . Twenty rupees is more than enough to take a colour laser print! Then, do you think that the other Unions will act like mere spectators? No way . . . So, better inform Police today itself.'

♥

The chief guest arrived exactly at two'o clock in the afternoon and magazine release function started with a prayer. Sheela prayed almost every God along with those girls! Subhash sat next to me proudly and the young girls told silly sweet nothings about him in between. Arun delivered the welcome speech and later invited me for the presidential address. What to say about him? I stood before them quite nervously.

'Dignitaries on the dais,' I couldn't remember even the names of my colleagues on the dais, 'Mr. Subhash, the new hero of Malayalam Cinema, colleagues and dear students. What is a magazine? It's a vault of memories . . . that you won't know now . . . You will feel it so dear after some time . . . when you might have left this institution . . . within a flash of a second, it can bring you back here . . . to this moment . . . Mr. Subhash . . . he is a hero now . . . But, he had also a bitter past, like you all, roaming around in this small village . . . What made him to reach here? A burning desire . . . to become a hero . . . He lived to it and that's why he is here with you today as our chief guest . . . The secret of success is constancy of purpose . . . It's time for you all to discover what your life's purpose is . . . Do it today and live up to it . . . Invent the dream in you . . . If a local boy can do that, why can't you?'

Subhash was listening to my words carefully and later I invited him to release the magazine. His father was sitting in the back row on the dais. Were there tears in his eyes?

After the magazine release, Subhash picked up the microphone and started sharing his wonderful experiences. He quoted some of my dialogues to motivate the students and within no time, he conquered their mind too!

Felicitations by other colleagues were also over and I announced for an open-forum with Subhash. Young boys and girls, they asked him wonderful questions and he too gave wonderful replies.

'You told . . . it was shot in forty days . . . Did you not fall in love with the heroine in the meantime?' one of my naughty students asked.

'Acting and love . . . they both are different,' Subhash laughed.

In the meantime, I made a wonderful friendship with his Dad. The function ended smoothly and Sheela Thomas felt very happy as the expected tension vanished in his divine bliss!

♥

The boys ran to us immediately after the Chief Guest and team had left.

'Sir . . . Please sanction for an immediate advance of Rs.5000/-,' Arun requested me.

'But, why?'

'We had to pay him Rs.5000/—for putting diesel in his car'

'You told me that he was coming to meet his parents? Then, why should we pay him? Impossible . . . You people are lying,' I got angry.

'No . . . Sir . . . We are telling the truth . . . Sir, this is the darker side of popularity . . . We had to pay for that!' they pleaded again.

'They may be right Premji,'Sheela Thomas supported them

'None can understand the Tinsel world!

♥

One week later, I met his Dad, drunk, in a bar hotel. I wanted to avoid him, but he didn't leave me.

'Hello Sir'

'Hello'

'Please join me,' poor man invited.

'O.K . . . But, the expense is mine . . . Is that O.K?'

'Double O.K.'

We had around two rounds of 'Mansion House' brandy in no time, and the intimacy got multiplied in unknown counts.

'Sir, if you don't mind, I would like to have a clarification?'

'Tell me'

'Did those boys pay Rs.5000/—to Subhash?'

'Yes . . . You are right . . . Everything has a price . . . this brandy . . . this chicken . . . his stardom . . . everything has a price.'

'Sorry . . . I couldn't get you?'

'Journalists . . . all magazine people . . . they can write anything on him . . . like . . . he was picked up by noted director Jose Samuel from thousands of applicants for audition . . . They can write anything they want . . . But, the documents of my house are still there, safe, in the state bank.'

'Sorry?'

'Premji . . . I had to pump Rupees one million to his throat to select him as the hero of his movie! Director! Thooo . . . ,' he spat on the granite floor, 'That producer didn't even pay a single rupee even-though the movie was a super hit . . . Bastards,' poor man started crying

'So sad'

'Subhash is a careless lad . . . See, how he spoiled his career by accepting all filthy roles in the name of commitments? Idiot! Now also, I have to pay him to for everything . . . from his expensive jeans . . . sexy T-shirts to diesel . . . His stupid burning desire,'he drank another double large without water. (This man is going to empty your ten day's salary, my inner conscious warned me!)

'Don't worry Sir . . . Everything will be alright . . . Anyway, he is a wonderful actor,' I tried to console him even-though I hadn't watched a single scene by him!

'That's O.K . . . But, what bothers me is . . . How can I be able to get my two daughters married . . . when every boy's parent is asking for 250 sovereigns of Gold . . . BMW 3 series car . . . Luxury flats in Kochi City . . . five acres of Rubber plantation as dowry! After all they are the sisters of Subhash . . . the hero! Everything has a price . . . everything . . . Every.'

October 25, 2011

9

Days Of Love

Royal Salute . . .

An unopened, Royal Salute bottle has been enjoying his extended life, inside our fridge for months . . . My dearest wife doesn't allow me to consume it! Every day, she forced me to say "Good Bye" to bottles, just by showing that expensive bottle, gifted by my brother-in-law . . . She stopped talking with him for that . . . What a silent revenge!

Never try to understand women! That is suicidal . . . Just love them . . . who said that? Man has life, only till the previous day of his marriage and the rest belongs to his wife till he takes rest forever! Man is born free, but . . . he is chained in married life! Is it the chain of love? Certainly, not always!

'Just for having a cup of tea, why should I have a tea estate!' a chronic bachelor friend made me laugh during a drinking session. Is that a joke?

Royal Salute . . . Like a seductress, she invites my attention every moment . . . God! Give me a chance to have her . . . at least one peg!

"Today I am very happy, come let's have three pegs . . . Today I feel very sad, come let's have another three more . . . Today I feel very bored, come let's have some more smalls . . . ,' my friends keep on inviting . . . What all reasons! Reasons! Every drunkard has innumerable reasons! Every drunkard is a very reasonable man! They will treat an artist with any type of liqueur . . . But, if you ask them just a small amount of money as a loan, or for some charity, there ends the friendship! This world is crazy to the core . . .

I thought of reading a novel after having a short nap in the afternoon . . . But words sound and feel quite unfamiliar . . . thirst . . . thirst . . . But, how?

Suddenly my elder son approached me, hiding something behind.

'What is that?'

"Nothing Dad . . . It's my progress card and I have to get it signed by you'

He handed over his progress card and a very good pen . . . Free flowing smooth pen . . . When you sign, you should never feel like signing . . . you have to give consent unknowingly . . . My son, quite intelligent you are! I was wild with anger after seeing his poor grades.

"Tell your teacher that . . . I will not sign . . .'

'Why Dad?'

"Why should I spend money for you? Especially, for poor grades like this? Now get lost from my sight . . .' Royal Salute . . . my sweet-heart . . . you still torment me . . . Is it an opportunity? Yes . . . Yes . . . Yes . . .

'Where is your mother?'

'She went to our aunt's house while you were sleeping'

"Sorry Dad, I am not that intelligent . . . I don't have enough capability.'

'What?'

'I am not capable, Dad . . . I am not that intelligent . . .'

'So you are not all capable . . . Did they teach about Human reproductive system?'

"Yes Dad'

"You are the one among those eighty million sperms, swam in search of that ovum in your mother's uterus . . . And you are the first among them to fuse with that . . . Now, tell me, do you have capability?'

"Yes . . . I have . . .'

'Tell it louder'

"Yes Daaaad'

"You are the one who lived like a King inside her womb for nine months without any problems . . . And born without any ailment . . . Now, do you have capability?'

'Yes . . . I am capable, Dad!'

"You still fight for your rights . . . And you try to implement your priorities by hook or crook . . . You win almost every time . . . So, do you have capability?'

"Yes . . . Dad!'

"Your father is an Engineer . . .'

"A writer too,' he interrupted in the middle.

"OK, your mother is a college lecturer having a Doctorate . . . the highest degree in our nation . . . Being our son, do you have enough genetic heredity of intelligence?'

"Yes Dad . . .'

"Now, answer my last question . . . Are you capable of doing anything?'

"Yes Dad . . . Yes Dad . . . You have imparted so much of faith . . . so much . . . Thank you Dad . . .'

I felt happiness deep within . . . But . . . My Royal Salute . . . My sweet-heart . . . the only opportunity is now!

"Boy, I am totally disappointed,' I told while walking towards the fridge . . .

"Please . . . Please don't drink . . . Dad . . . ,' my son started pleading.

'What is the point feeding idiots like you? Let me die . . . sure . . . that doesn't affect you,' I was busy opening the bottle.

"Daaaad . . . pleaaaaaaaaase don't drink . . . You know . . . if you drink, your liver, the largest organ in your body, will swell . . . it is not good for your health . . .'

"Let it swell . . . so what? I don't care . . . let me die . . . let me die . . . ,' I told while enjoying the sweet odour of Royal Salute . . . She filled my lungs with great happiness . . .

Suddenly, my son hugged me tightly, crying.

"Dad . . . you can drink as you like . . . 'Let me die' . . . 'Let me die' . . . you say every moment . . . Dad, you have nothing to lose . . . But, I have a lot . . . Dad . . . If you die, I will become fatherless . . . Tell me, to whom will I share my intense secrets . . . Tell me, who will protect me in my tough times? Who will love me more than you? You have nothing to lose, Dad . . . But, I have a lot to lose . . . we have a lot . . . Please don't drink, Dad . . . Please . . . ,' he caught hold of the bottle and within no time, it was in his hands . . . I didn't offer any resistance . . . I still cannot believe that . . . I didn't offer any resistance.

"Dad, we will grow a water-plant in it,' he told while pouring down her in the wash basin, tears rolling down his eyes. 'Every moment, it will make me remember, Dad . . . I am capable . . . Capable of doing anything . . .'

In a quick move, my wife entered into the house and hugged him tightly . . . Was she hiding somewhere?

'I am capable of doing anything . . . Mom . . . I will not hurt you anymore . . . I promise' . . .

She couldn't control her tears . . . I was standing there just like a statue made of salt . . . please don't cry . . . You may dissolve me away . . .

She hugged me tightly and planted a kiss on my lips . . .

'What are you doing? The boy will see . . .'

"Let him see . . . Who cares? I got my lover back . . . back in the days of love . . .'

"Home . . . happy home,' my younger son started singing a nursery rhyme while getting up from his afternoon nap . . .

O! My Royal Salute!

July 09, 2011

10

Sensational News

It was around eight'o clock in the morning and the Railway canteen looked almost empty. Twelve year old Ayyappa Das—a neatly dressed, bit dark, Telugu boy entered in quite happily.

'What would you like have today?' waiter asked.

'One plate Iddly* Sambhar*, and two sets parcel,' he answered coolly in an alien language . . . a perfect blend of Malayalam, Tamil and Telugu . . .

Ayyappa Das carefully dipped one small iddli in hot sambhar and started eating very slowly. It resembled a practical demonstration: how to eat!

'Only those who know real hunger can eat like this,' a Sergeant, belonging to Railway Protection Force, opined. He was watching him carefully, from the very moment he had entered in.

'Sir . . . he is seen here for the last two weeks . . . Nobody has any idea about him . . . like from where does he come . . . or what does he do?' the Railway canteen owner told the Sargent in Malayalam . . . 'Quite mysterious'

'Will he come tomorrow?'

'I think so'

Ayyappa Das collected the parcel and handed over a five hundred rupee note. The boy collected the balance and left the canteen. Sergeant's face grew darker and darker.

♥

Sixty eight year old Krishnan Namboodiri was watching BBC News, after finishing the morning duties, inside that two bedroom flat. The slanting rays of the morning Sun fell on his wrinkle-free face, which gave him an additional aura. Devaki Antharjanam, his beloved wife, was bedridden inside, as steel rods were inserted in her left leg due to multiple fractures. She needed someone's help always.

'Thanks to painkillers,' Namboodiri told himself as she was sleeping peacefully when he had a quick glance through the half closed door.

'Good Morning . . . Namboodiri Sir,' I greeted him warmly.

'Good Morning . . . Premji . . . Today is a holiday for you, isn't it?'

'Yes Sir . . . one of the state ministers is no more'

'That is the one and only advantage you get from a politician . . . that too after his death!' he said while laughing.

'How is Madam today?'

'Much better'

Suddenly a twenty five year old beauty entered in without even asking for permission.

'Pardon me Madam . . . I am afraid . . . I don't know . . . ,' Namboodiri stopped abruptly.

'Don't worry Sir . . . Premji knows me'

'Sir . . . She is Ms. Sangeetha . . . a noted journalist by profession . . . ,' I introduced her. 'She has a couple of great stories in her credit and one of them lead to the political exile of some leaders,'

'Please . . . take your seat Madam,' he welcomed her. 'Premji, you talk with her and in the mean time I will prepare some coffee'

'No need of it . . . Sir, where is that boy?' her voice was not that pleasing.

'Who?'

'I don't know his name,'

'O . . . Ayyappa Das . . . He has gone for tuition . . . without knowing Malayalam, it's not easy for him to survive here in Kerala'

'Don't you know that child labour is a criminal offense?' she was getting aggressive.

'What offense? I am his local guardian . . . Let me ask you a very simple question . . .

Who are you?'

'I am Sangeetha. We run a non-profit organization named 'M&K,' partnered with Childline*. We got a complaint from a very reliable source . . .' she replied, that too her temper was steaming up!

'Will you please explain me what is Childline?' Namboodiri asked.

'We support children . . . We save them from all sorts of exploitations,'

'What kind of children?'

'Children who live on the street with their families and often work on the street . . . There may be children from migrated families, or temporarily migrated and are likely to go back to their homes. Children who live on the street by themselves or in groups and have remote access or contact with their families in the villages. Some children travel to the cities for the day or periods of time to work and then return to their villages. Children who have no ties to their families such as orphans, refugees and runaways,' she started talking quite fast as if recorded in her soul!

'He doesn't belong to any of these,' Namboodiri declared openly in the middle.

'Is he your son?'

'No.'

'Is he your adopted son?'

'Yes'

'Do you have any substantial evidences with you now?'

'No'

'What?'

'What is wrong in helping a child?' Namboodiri was getting confused.

'Sir . . . There is nothing wrong in helping a child . . . But, what you do now is illegal . . . I am so sorry . . . we are be forced to lodge a complaint against you,' she told her clear-cut decision.

'Sangeetha . . . Why do you want to insult a reputed man and his bedridden wife, without even knowing the truth?' I asked

'What truth? Premji . . . Such people will have a million truths to say! Everyone wants someone to relieve his or her burdens . . . Unfortunately children are the victims,' there was contempt projected in her voice.

'Madam, are you bold enough to go Hyderabad along with Premji? You can go by the morning flight . . . and come back in the evening flight . . . don't worry . . . I will bear the expenses . . .' Namboodiri asked her politely though he was burning with anger.

'For what?'

'To know the truth . . . the truth . . . brighter than millions of Suns,'

'Yes,' she said aloud as her boldness was deep hurt!

♥

Anuradha Menon was waiting there in Hyderabad Airport with her white Maruti van.

'Hello Premji,' she hugged me tightly.

'Hi Anu . . . How are you?'

'We are fine,' then she extended her hand towards Sangeetha.

Sangeetha stood motionless for a moment . . . she couldn't believe her eyes . . .

'Anuradha Menon . . . Anuradha Menon,'

'Do you know me?'

'Yes . . . Madam . . . I admire you . . . from my college days,' Sangeetha replied with lot of admiration.

Sangeetha was almost silent during the whole journey. It took almost forty minutes to enter into the compounds of 'Swathantra' (the freed), the headquarters of an NGO, helping destitute women and children. The tall buildings made of mud resembled the simplicity of life there. Constructions were still going on.

'Mud is stronger than concrete . . . It was the building material of the past . . . future too!' Anuradha Menon told. 'Sangeetha . . . This place was donated by Devaki ji'

'Who is that . . . Madam?' Sangeetha asked.

'The better-half of Krishnan Ji'

'Krishnan Ji?'

'Yes . . . He only sent you here . . .' Sangeetha felt somewhat guilty . . .

'Premji,' Anuradha Menon tossed the van key to me, 'Go and meet your old friends'

♥

'Krishnan Ji was the Chief Editor of 'Jwaala . . . the flame,' one of the top circulated dailies in Telugu. He was the only man who stood with us when we started saving women and children from brothels . . . His people protected us day and night from their gangsters . . . He arranged for loans for us . . . He is our one and only surety other than God!' Anuradha Menon told her while walking through their campus.

'But, only very few know that'

'Good Morning Deedi*,' children, who were studying under a tree, greeted her warmly.

'A very Good Morning,' she cheered them up. 'I will clear your doubts in the evening'

'Wonderful kids . . . Deedi,' Sangeetha told.

'None of them knows their father . . . So sad,'

'Deedi . . . You didn't say anything about Ayyappa Das?'

'We are going to meet his mother,' Anuradha said calmly.

There . . . she was lying inside a well-ventilated room . . . her hands and legs resembled twigs in the winter . . . her eyeballs were like two burnt out stars . . . Yes . . . she was the star of so many 'fleshy dream nights! And a cheap rate prostitute in India doesn't have the guts and right to ask her customer to wear a condom!

'Banu . . . how are you today?' Anuradha asked.

'I am so tired . . . Deedi . . . I can't even move my fingers,' a pale voice escaped from a drum ribbed with two hundred and six bones . . .

'See . . . Ayyappan has sent presents for you through Sangeetha . . . Cakes . . . Christmas cakes . . . We will cut them in the evening,' Anurandha introduced her.

'Madam, how is he?' the feeble woman asked Sangeetha in Tamil.

'He is fine,' Sangeetha told.

'Does he eat anything? Does he study well? Do you teach him? Will he come to meet me?'

'Yes . . . he misses you a lot,' she prepared herself to tell a series of lies . . .

'She is counting her days . . . slim disease eats away her life like hungry maggots,' Anuradha told while returning.

'Slim disease . . . what is that?' Sangeetha asked.

'H.I.V'

♥

Ayyappa Das was away at school when we reached his home on the very next day.

'Sir . . . I am really sorry,' Sangeetha didn't feel like talking more as her soul was bruised with guilt.

'Don't worry . . . experiences strengthen life,' Namboodiri told her.

'I know . . . Sir'

'Sangeetha, why don't you write about Anuradha Menon and 'swathantra'?' I asked.

'That's a wonderful idea . . . Premji . . . I will write about our trip to Hyderabad . . . Sure . . . I will write about Ayyappa Das too,' Sangeetha was really exhilarated.

'I will not allow that,' Namboodiri's voice raised above all.

'But, Sir?' Sangeetha was perplexed.

'You have every right to write about Anuradha and Swathantra . . . that's sensible journalism . . . But . . . you have no right to write about Ayyappa Das . . . If you do that . . . that's called sensational journalism . . . A journalist is not a hunter . . . but a fighter . . . Do have empathy on anything or anyone . . . about whom you write,' Namboodiri told, with an unexpected glow on his face.

'I understand . . . Sir,' Sangeetha told.

'Wrong information, shared with the public, can cripple many lives . . . Clarifications on the next editions do nothing,'

'I understand . . . Sir'

'She passed away yesterday evening'

'I understand . . . Sir'

December 26, 2011

11

Love Is A Double Edged Sword

Before getting the status of 'Silicon Valley of India,' Bangalore City was known as 'pensioner's paradise'. My uncle too migrated there after retirement and he opened a telephone booth with fourteen lines to get out of boredom after a quick honeymoon with the city. He is very fond of me and I use to visit him regularly. But, he was intelligent enough to take dealerships of almost all cellular phone providers at the very starting of cell-phone boom in India. There, I met him . . . Veer Singh Bahadur, a Gurkha from Nepal. He was working as a security man in a large women's hostel where lot of young girls working in IT sector used to stay. He is a well-built young man of five feet two inches height. An innocent smile was hidden behind his eyes always.

'Sir, where is Gopi Sab?' he asked me one day while I was sitting in the cash counter.

'Uncle has gone out Veer Singh . . . Tell me the matter'

'I need some re-charge coupons for those girls . . . Gopi Sab used to give them on credit base,' he told quite innocently. I checked up the matter with my uncle through mobile phone and issued them happily.

♥

'Prem, if I keep Rupees one million on that table and tell him to take care of it . . . then I can go for a world tour peacefully . . . You know, the money will be safe, remain untouched, when I return . . . That's the belief I have on Veer Singh . . . He is a Gurkha . . . embodiment of faith,' my uncle told in that evening.

'Yes . . . I know'

'If a man says he is not afraid of dying, he is either lying or is a Gurkha'. I remembered the famous quote by Former Chief of staff of the Indian Army, Field Marshal Sam Manekshaw.

Three days later, I met Veer Singh Bahadur again at Bangalore Railway station.

'Premji Sab, I think you are going back to Trivandrum'

'Yes, Veer Singh'

'Even, I am going back . . . Shadi . . . Sab . . . Shadi* . . . I am going to get married next week.'

'Congratulations in advance Bahadur . . . Is it a love marriage?'I started kidding him.

'No Sab . . . it happens only in movies,'he replied shyly.

'But, I know that you are in love . . . So, when will you return?

'You are very naughty, Sab . . . I will return only after two months Sab'

♥

I was thinking about him while traveling in the moving train. Gurkhas . . . they work in India as trusted security men from the times of British Raj. Born fighters they are! Gurkha regiment is one of the most privileged regiment of Indian army. Why do they work in India for cheap wages? For them, it is a great sum as the money value of Indian Currency is almost double than that of Nepal's currency! So it is a profitable occupation. But, new generation security cameras are a real threat to them. But, machines don't have that something . . . Guts . . . Courage . . .

♥

Again I had to be there in Bangalore for a week to look after the business as my uncle was on tour to Thailand with his family. These new generation companies are so cunning, they give more and more gifts to get more and more business. Veer Bahadur came to our shop to get some more recharge coupons.

'How is your new life?' I asked.

'What life, Sab? She is there and I am here,' he replied in a sad tone . . .

His pain is known to me as Kerala has the highest number of 'Gulf widows'. Husbands return to Gulf weeks after marriages. Who knows when they will return! Veer Bahadur has to spend another ten months to meet his young wife. And the saddest thing was . . . he had to spend twenty four hours guarding very sexy girls . . . that too in the cool climate of Bangalore . . . What a punishment! God! Poor guy lived like a drained soul.

'Sab, will you please do me one favour?'

'Tell me, Veer Singh'

'Sab, just before leaving for Bangalore, I presented her a new mobile phone so that I can talk to her twice in a week. There are no land phone lines in our village. But, our Matron Madam doesn't allow me to go out frequently. And when Parbati, my wife, calls, Madam doesn't allow me talking more than a minute.'

'It's a painful situation Bahadur . . . Your Madam is very cruel . . . tell her to fall in love with someone.'

'You can only help me, Sab,' he told while taking out an old NOKIA handset from his khaki uniform. 'One of the kind girls gifted me this . . . but . . . this is of no use without a SIM card. I don't have a passport or any identity cards . . . but, you can provide me one SIM card.'

'That's not possible Veer Singh . . . it's against the law. If anything happens, uncle will have to go to jail,' I had to deny his request painfully

'It's OK Sab . . . Forgive me . . . ,' he said while leaving hopelessly.

Poor man . . . I felt very sad . . .

♥

Uncle and family landed after two days. Veer Bahadur helped me in packing up some household articles that I purchased from Bangalore. My wife was already fed up of my frequent trips to Bangalore. Casual leaves . . . half pay leaves . . . and almost all forms of leaves were over . . . My Principal was showing his cruelty as scores of green ink on my columns in the office attendance register. My wife too started scratching with her sharp nails! Just to console her, I had to invest more money on Saris, Churidars, nail polishes . . . no Gold . . . it's unthinkable . . . Woman's world is so queer! The life of a man ends on the previous night of his marriage!

'Krrning . . . Krrning.'

Suddenly Veer Singh pulled out a mobile phone from his pocket. His face started glowing like a Khukri* (the razor sharp knife used by them) on broad Sunlight . . . happiness of a small boy, having a chocolate for the first time in life . . .

'It's Parbati . . . Sab . . .'

Poor guy was kissing the handset . . . Even I too felt very happy seeing the lover in him . . . O! What exhilaration! Love is sweet madness . . .

He talked with her for nearly three minutes in hiding . . .

'Veer Singh, how did you manage to get a SIM card?'

'Sab, if you have money, you can get anything in Bangalore,' he said proudly.

'So you are happy . . . Now you can tell her sweet nothings in the nights too.'

'You are really naughty, Sab,' he told while laughing shyly.

♥

I had a routine call from my uncle next week.

'Prem, I have sad news to share with you'

'Please tell me, uncle'

'Veer Bahadur is in jail'

'What?'

'Yes . . . he is in jail . . . Anti-terrorist squad of Karnataka state, along with National security agencies had arrested him. It was a combined operation'

'Uncle . . . How can a poor man be labeled as a terrorist?'

'This is the same question even I had asked myself'

'Quite embarrassing . . . Does he have any connections with Maoists of Nepal?'

'No'

'Then why?'

'He was using a SIM card that was under scanner of security agencies. It was one among those used by the terrorists who were behind some serial bomb blasts in Bangalore.'

'Unbelievable!'

'Then what was Veer Bahadur's version?'

'He says that he got it from the footpath. He won't able to get out even after twenty years. Life is gone!'

'He is telling the truth.'

'How do you know that?'

'A Gurkha will never tell lie . . . especially a Gurkha in love'

My mind is imprisoned along with him since then . . .

*Marriage . . .

August 25, 2011

12

FATHER

NOW-A-DAYS, I LOVE FRIDAYS very much! Because, it is on Fridays we reunite as a family again, that too after four days of separation! Our children live with their grandma. Wife and I, we work at different places, some two hundred kilometers apart from them. Life is like that! And if you wish to be happy in life, accept it as it is!

It was again a Friday, nearly one month back . . . I had been waiting for my wife at Trivandrum Railway station since around six thirty in the evening. Three evening tabloids made the 'waiting' joyful. I love to read tabloids as they give wonderful ideas for any writer! I settled on to one of the long chairs in the platform. Nobody dared to sit near me as my mustache and body language resembles to that of a high ranking Police official, except mosquitoes and bugs! A boon in disguise!

Sometimes, reading is a very dirty habit! Her train arrived and people scattered away like waves receding to the sea after a Tsunami. And the funniest thing was . . . I was not all aware of the surroundings, except an article written by my friend, about increasing rate of alcoholic addiction among call girls! Customers seemed to be crazy of making them being drunk and having violent sex with 'sweat smelling' night Jasmines! What an extensive research he had done for that report!

'Great!'

'Really great!' my wife shook me back to senses. 'If I was there in the position of his wife, I would have registered a petition for divorce by now'

'I am sorry . . . Come . . . Shall we have a cup of coffee?' (Crazy girl was not all caring for me!) 'What shall we get for the children?' I tried to change the subject.

'Let's go home as early as possible . . . Kids might sleep off,' the deep longing of a mother to hug her kids was clear in her voice.

'I won't get even a hug tonight . . . you bastard!' I cursed the tabloid reporter.

♥

Usually, I used to listen to her wonderful stories during those one hour long bus journeys. Writers are crazy people, they may find a poem or a story even when their dear and near are in death bed! She was totally silent on that Friday, just by burying herself deep into those three tabloids.

'Tonight is going to be another fasting night!' I cursed the woman from whom I purchased those tabloids and closed my eyes. I was not blessed with sleep, how could I? The scent of a 'dear woman' can throw any man to sweet madness, that too after some days of separation!

'Premji . . . did you see this?'

'What?'

'A teenage girl died, on the spot, hit by a car . . . Very near to our house . . . You know her family very well'

'No . . . I didn't'

'How will you see that . . . when doing research on call girls?' her temper was not going to subside!

♥

I was standing in front of that vegetable shop, immediately opposite to my friend's Photostat shop, on the next day morning. The steel pipes which supported his veranda were bent and the compound wall of the house, next to his shop looked demolished by a massive impact!

'Hi . . . Premji,' Sam touched my shoulders.

'Hi . . . Sam'

Every shop remained closed that day in honour of the departed girl. Sam rolled up the shutters and started taking some photocopies, paying homage to her.

'Premji . . . usually, she comes inside when she accompanied her friends to take photocopies of class notes . . . but . . . yesterday, she just waited outside . . . and that bastard rammed his car on to her . . . poor girl was crushed in between the car and that wall . . . ,' he pointed toward the broken wall where red ants were still moving around her semi-dried blood . . . blue in colour . . .

'Luckily, I was saved as we used to stand there during free time'

'Was he drunk?'

'That bastard . . . was full tight! Heavily drunk . . . you know . . . he lost control while preparing a drink . . . that too while driving! And that son of a bitch, escaped during that confusion,'

'Sam . . . One of his relatives . . . a policeman . . . tried to remove alcohol bottles from the car, it seems . . . ,' I tried to share a piece of information.

'He tried . . . but . . . he was caught ready-handed by our youngsters . . . they bashed him to pulp! Bastard! Lawmakers are bloody lawbreakers most of the times . . .'

♥

Sam was busy sticking those photocopies on walls. Her spotless innocent face on them remains as an everlasting scar in my mind.

'Premji . . . I couldn't sleep a single moment yesterday . . . Whenever I tried to close my eyes, I could see her vomiting blood by calling 'Achchaaa . . . (faaather . . .)' . . . Just three times . . . she vomited blood and closed her eyes . . . she was only . . . just fifteen . . . My hands still smell her blood . . . ,' Sam smelled the gum-clad right hand.

'Such bastards have to be thrown behind the bars for a minimum of fourteen years . . . rigorous imprisonment'

'Yes . . . bastards have to sweat out even their bones!' Sam told out his solidarity.

Suddenly an ambulance appeared on the main road.

'She is back,' Sam told painfully.

♥

Forty five year old Sugathan and his wife cried aloud as their one and only child Meena slept forever, on a narrow desk, decorated with expensive flowers which she couldn't even have imagined when she was alive. Her face, unharmed, resembled another red Rose and her crushed bosom remained like a trough where her pains were deep buried!

'Madam, where shall I dig the grave?' Johnson, the gravedigger, asked our local body member politely.

That simple question pierced everyone's mind like a harpoon! She walked around the shack, two or three times, to find a suitable place. But, unfortunately she was not successful in that attempt as Sugathan had only seven hundred square-feet of land as that of his own! That too, land without any document!

'There is no space at all . . . So . . . shall we bury her inside the house,' she asked us, totally confused.

'Madam . . . we can bury her, here,' gravedigger Johnson suggested, pointing towards the door-steps in front of that thatched shack. 'But, it won't be possible to get out of the house without crossing her grave!' he felt so sad as if someone had punctured his heart forever.

Boys from the local Arts and Sports Club distributed bread and black coffee to people when burial was over. Sam vomited violently as if he had drunk blood! Blue blood! All I could do was just rubbing his back!

Our local body member tried to give a five hundred rupee note to gravedigger Johnson.

'Madam . . . I too am a father . . . of two girls . . . please,' he denied that with honour.

♥

Untimely rains are the harbingers of danger! A rootless, dried up tree fell on the compound wall of our home and stray dogs started entering in from the nearby beach.

'European tourists are really crazy . . . they feed all stray dogs . . . ,' my wife told out of anger while pelting a stone.

Sugathan was also among the masons as a helper. His bearded face resembled that of a ghost, but his lifeless eyes were burning with anger . . . Where did his lust for life vanish?

♥

Five months back . . . It a fine morning in April and I was busy surfing through poetfreak, reading the poems of Nimal. Nearly two thousand poems . . . O! This man is a thought-battery! I was fluttering like a thirsty butterfly through the untouched flowers!

'Papa . . . somebody is out there to meet you,' my younger son announced.

Sugathan and his beautiful daughter Meena were standing at the doorstep.

'Come in,' I welcomed them.

'No need Sir . . . We will stand here,' the poor man in Sugathan desperately trying to satisfy his ego!

'That, I will decide . . . come inside'

'As you wish,' he told while entering in. 'Sir, I need your valuable advice'

'O.K. What's the matter?'

'Sir . . . Immediately after the completion of SSLC, my daughter Meena plans to join a Polytechnic College for technical education,' Sugathan said polietly. 'Someone told her that you work in a polytechnic . . . Sir, can I afford it?'

'Her decision is right . . . She can learn engineering, absolutely free of cost . . . under fee waiver schemes,'I told confidently.

Meena smiled happily as someone in the world had accepted her decision. Acceptance, that's the only thing the whole world is longing for!

'Will she get a job after that?' Sugathan asked innocently as every father's mind is like an open hearth, where fire kindles mercilessly . . . especially parents of poor young girls!

'That depends on the course she selects and her academic excellence later,' I replied. 'Meena, which branch would you like to learn?'

'Automobile Engineering,' she said boldly.

'Meena . . . it's a branch meant for boys! Why do you want to learn it?' I couldn't hide my anxieties.

'Sir, that doesn't matter . . . I know that you can easily put me inside of some huge vehicle dealerships as a front office executive or as a service advisor,' she replied confidently. 'Moreover, I can clear my doubts when you are at home'

'Can you speak in English fluently?'

'Why not! It takes just two months to learn English for anybody who knows his or her mother-tongue better!' Meena replied with enthusiasm. Such a confident girl is a real blessing to any father!

♥

Sugathan was making cement mortar, all alone, and the spade vanished inside the sand heap as if he was digging a grave! So powerful were the strokes!

'Eyy . . . Sugathan . . . what are you doing? We have to stand here . . . don't you see Cement fly up?' Chandran, the chief mason shouted.

Sugathan was not even aware of that and he continued the mixing. At last, the masons washed their hands and legs as it was nearing lunch time.

'Sugathan, come let's go,' the chief mason said.

'You please proceed . . . I am not feeling hungry'

'O.K . . . but, don't spoil your health'

'No problem . . . hunger is nothing new to me,' Sugathan lit a Beedi. (locally made cigarette)

It's burning end brightened like the morning sun . . . So Red in coluor . . . like his peace-less mind . . . While he was taking the nicotine smoke inside with enormous passion, I walked near to him.

'Sugathan . . . Come . . . let's have something from my home,' I invited him for food.

'Premji Sir . . . I am not feeling hungry at all . . . You know . . . He started driving Cars again,'

'Who?'

'That bastard, who killed my daughter . . . He crippled three others earlier because of his drunken driving . . . but, my . . . one and only daughter,' poor man started crying. 'I could have looked her after . . . if at least, some life was left on her body . . . Sir, we have no point in continuing this life,'

'I know . . . Didn't they cancel his driving license?' I asked.

'License . . . for him? Authorities are heartless bastards! He has many driving licenses in different names! Money can do wonders! Money!'

'You are right . . . These bastards have to be put behind the bars for life imprisonment,' I told out of anger.

'That's not enough . . . Sir, do you know something . . . yesterday night, they bashed up those boys who hit that policeman who tried to remove liquor bottles from that car,'

'Who did that?'

'Policemen . . . it seems . . . it's a warning . . . none should touch a Policeman though his doings are wrong!'

'Are we going through another emergency?'

'I don't know . . . But . . . He should never be allowed to touch the steering wheel again . . . I have to make five thousand rupees as early as possible,'

'You skip meals for that?'

'Yes . . . I have nothing to sell . . . All I know is . . . I need that much money immediately . . . I have some twenty thousand rupees with me . . . given by her friends . . . And they have agreed to do that, for rupees twenty five thousand though their rate is fifty thousand . . . They also gave me a discount of twenty five thousands . . . they too have sisters,' Sugathan said boisterously.

'Who are they?'

'The gangsters form Fort Cochin . . . They have undertaken a 'quotation work' for me to crush his hands with iron bars . . . that he should beg for a living . . . they will powder his finger bones . . . It should be a lesson to the world . . . ,' his eyes started glowing like a red-hot Beedi tip!

'Papa . . . are you not coming for food?' my elder son came near running and asked.

'I am coming,' he ran back contended. 'It should be a lesson . . . it should be,' I told myself.

'My wife is suffering from heavy depression now . . . I am not sure whether she would be alive when I return home . . . who knows whether she might recover just by seeing him begging . . . ,' poor man started crying silently.

'Papa,' the boy started shouting again.

'Sugathan, I will pay the rest,' I told him calmly . . .

'Papa . . . Are you not coming for food?' I heard a girl child calling aloud!

December 18, 2011

13

Holy Brothers

As THE PART OF my career, we were forced to live in that small town in central Kerala for some time. Our house owner Johnychayan was quite a simple man, working as military nurse in Oman. When I met him for the first time, he was really happy to give his house for rent. I was a Government employee and that time we didn't have any kids. What a funny reason to select a tenant!

'Premji, all I need from you both . . . just keep my house neat and tidy,' he told.

'Sir, what about rent?'

'Actually, I have to pay you something to keep my house tidy!' he said jovially. 'Here is my account number,' he handed over a small piece of paper. 'Whatever amount is affordable by you, put it in my account . . . monthly . . . bimonthly or as you like.'

What an offer . . . God!

'Sir . . . When shall we write the agreement?'

'No need of an agreement, Premji . . . I know . . . you are a gentleman. See, I am not going to cut my telephone land-line. You can use that too,' he told while laughing.'

He was waiting for someone whom he could believe to the core and of course, we were the chosen people. He and his family went back on the very next week. They would be back only after five years . . . five years . . . We were very happy to live in such a gentleman's house.

♥

There was a huge picture of Jesus in the drawing room and I used to light candles on important occasions like Christmas, Easter etc. My wife used to keep candles there whenever there was a power-cut! She kept her personal deities inside another room . . . Hindu Gods and Goddesses . . .

My wife was all alone in day time, watching TV while knitting something. That was her daily routine except on holidays. Then one day, Thresya Chechi around 55, our next door neighbor and elder sister of our house owner Johnychayan, visited her. She was warmly welcomed by my wife.

'Daughter, this is really nice,' Thresya Chechi congratulated my wife after inspecting the small sweater my wife had knitted. 'Expecting someone?'she started kidding.

'No'

'Now-a-days, every girl has infertility problems . . . Why girls alone? Boys too . . . Dirty food habits . . . You don't worry daughter . . . He will bless you soon' . . . Jesus smiled at them from the picture on the wall. They talked about everything under the Sun and at last they became very close friends.

♥

My wife told me the entire episode in the evening.

'That's a good development . . . Thresya Chechi has nothing to do in day time'

'Even I too think so, Premji'

♥

Thresya Chechi became a frequent visitor and everyday the conversation used to end up in Jesus. She had more than a million tongues to talk about Jesus and his miracles. One evening, my wife showed me a fresh copy of Bible.

'Who gave it?'

'Thresya Chechi presented this to me'

'This is an expensive copy. Keep it with care.'

♥

Ours is a small family and we used to complete all cooking jobs before 8'O clock. She used to make boiled rice and break-fast and I, all curries. On the very next day, when I had left for office, Thresya Chechi appeared with a pleasant smile. They both started talking casually.

'Daughter, did you start reading Bible?'

'I went through proverbs . . . read one or two pages.'

'Praise the Lord . . . That's interesting . . . First of all . . . you have to complete New Testament . . . That tells the life and miracles of my Lord . . . Jesus'

'I will do it . . . Chechi'

♥

Thresya Chechi again appeared on the same time next day and she started asking objective questions based on new testament. My wife answered all as she read it the last day afternoon by sacrificing her afternoon sleep.

'Great improvement . . . Congratulations my daughter,' Thresya Chechi was contented. 'Tomorrow Psalms'. She then gave her new home works based on Bible and my wife was fed of Thresya Chechi's Bible home tuition!

♥

'Premji, tell me a way out.'

'Simple . . . You read 'Song of songs' tonight . . . I too want to listen.'

♥

Thresya Chechi was very uneasy on the next day.

'Who told you read that?'Thresya Chechi asked.

'My husband . . . He says . . . Song of Songs is the spiritual communion of human soul and Holy Spirit'

Thresya Chechi became quite very unhappy!

♥

Three days later, our telephone started ringing in the night. Our house owner Johnychayan was on the other end, from Oman. It seems, he got a call from Thresya Chechi to vacate us as early as possible from his house. She won't be able to tolerate two infidels staying in her brother's house!

'Premji, what happened? Did she start playing her cards on your wife?' Johnychayan asked.

'Yes, Bible tuitions were going on!'

'Then how did it come to an abrupt end?'

'Johnychaya . . . What to say? My wife was really fed of her Bible tuition . . . So, one day, she visited Thresya Chechi's home and presented her a copy of Hindu Scripture: Bhagavad Gita (Song divine) . . . A small copy worth just ten rupees! She asked Thresya Chechi to read the first chapter that day . . . so that they could discuss that chapter on the very next day.'

'Premji . . . Your wife is an intelligent girl . . . please tell her my congratulations . . . ,' Johnychayan couldn't control his laughing. 'From the past five years, my house has been closed . . . Only because of her tuitions . . . She is a member of some local Ministry now . . . Only one

Jesus . . . countless Ministries! She keeps on fishing and I keep on suffering,'he laughed again.

'Johnychaya, are you not worried?'

'Premji . . . Why should I worry when Jesus protects me? In Bhagavad Gita, Lord Krishna says . . . perform your Karma . . . never think of the reward . . . My Lord Jesus says: 'sacrifice!' Premji . . . you know . . . 'Good Karma and sacrifice,' these words are synonymous! And the reward is eternal happiness! Peace! Unfortunately, my sister doesn't understand this simple truth. Why, my sister alone? . . . almost everyone, irrespective of religions!'

I could feel the pain of Jesus and Krishna in his voice . . . Holy brothers . . .

July 03, 2011

14

MEDI'SIN'

FIFTEEN YEARS BACK . . .

I had to resign from that prestigious company during my younger sister's marriage. Everyone asked my parents: 'Why did he do that?' Dad was fed up of this repeated question and he stopped talking to me. There was another reason too: I was one of the most eligible bachelors of our village! A jobless bachelor is mere waste!

Just for pass time, all I could do was reading books. I read every precious book from our local library. Joy, the librarian, he was my only friend. We used to smoke packets of Wills and discuss everything under the Sun. Then 'he' came, a very handsome guy, in search books.

'Premji, Dr. Sunil . . . the new doctor in 'SB Hospital,' Joy introduced him. 'Doctor, this is Premji . . . Ex-sales engineer!'

'Ex?'

'Yes doctor . . . jobless at present!' Joy teased me.

Two bachelors of same age . . . Sunil and I . . . We became very close friends in no time and I used to visit his quarters in the evenings. One day, I presented him a copy of my first book, a collection of short stories in Malayalam. He read the whole book in that night itself. He wrote and gave a letter of appreciation on the very next day. It was the first appreciation for writing, in writing, in my life. That evening, we were talking about the alarming rate of sterility among women who reside in the cities.

'Premji, I like the way you write stories . . . Now, I am going to tell you story . . . someday, in future, you can write it'

'That's interesting Doc!'

'Two years back . . . we were working as House Surgeons at our Medical College . . . One night, we . . . me, my friend Sajeev and his girlfriend Anita . . . were sitting in the casualty. Suddenly Anita started playing with the surgical cotton kept on the table.

'Anita, please don't touch it . . . It's sterile.'

'I know it's sterile . . . But, you are not sterile!'

Then Sajeev and Anita burst into laughter . . . I wanted to kill that bastard that moment itself . . . They went on laughing . . .

'Sajeev, what kind of idiot are you . . . telling intimate secrets to women? She will tell the entire college . . . Shit,' I started scolding him.

'Anita, did you tell that to anyone?'Sajeev enquired.

'No'

'You better stick on to that 'No' . . . Otherwise, I will divorce you . . . Understand.'

'Divorce . . . even before marriage! That's great,'she laughed.

'Doc . . . then, why did they laugh at you?'I asked.

'I am not sterile, Premji'

'That means?'

'I have two sons,'he told in pain.

'Doc . . . What are you saying? You are still a bachelor!'

'So what! Premji, you are an engineer . . . You won't understand the plight of a Medical student . . . Every Medical student . . . he or she has to be the most obedient to all Professors . . . otherwise Bachelor of Medicine will remain only as a dream.'

'That's there even in Engineering Colleges'

'Not up to our standards.'

'May be . . . then Doc.'

'One day, I bunked the morning classes and was sleeping nicely in the hostel . . . Then somebody knocked on the door . . . Which bastard is that not allowing me to sleep? Our Department Head's personal peon was standing outside.

'Anything important, Rajettan?'

'HOD wants to meet you . . . right now'

Jumped into jeans, I ran behind him. HOD was busy reading some medical journals.

'Good Morning . . . Sir.'

'Morning . . . Why did you bunk the classes?'

'Not feeling well . . . Sir,' I told a lie that he understood in no time.

'Sunil . . . You are in the final year . . . So, be careful.'

He was silent for a moment . . .

'Now . . . Go . . . Get it,' HOD told while handing over a small glass bottle . . .

I rushed out with the bottle. Peon Rajettan was standing outside . . . He was smiling . . .

'Rajettan, what is happening around?'

'Nothing man . . . A family is under treatment in our infertility clinic . . . Her husband was in Dubai for the past 12 years . . . His balls are dried up of the hot Sun . . . She is so beautiful . . . You are her ideal match . . . Your HOD has a great sense of beauty!' he started teasing me again.

Back in hostel, I was busy searching for some porn books . . . At last I got couple of copies of 'Fantasy' . . . Lovely pictures . . . beautiful stories . . . but . . . but . . .

'How come you are so late?'HOD asked in anger.

'Sir . . . tension.'

'What tension? Now . . . out.'

He kicked me out mercilessly and walked away with the bottle . . . Millions of fighters were swimming towards the unknown destination! God! My life . . . my life . . .

After nine months, one day Rajettan came in search of me again. I stood before my HOD like a lamb before a butcher.

'Boy, Congratulations . . . Now you are a proud father of two young boys,'he told . . .

'Sir?'

'Twins'

'Sir, can I see them at least once?'

'Sorry . . . No . . . It's against medical ethics.'

'Sir . . . please . . . only once,'I started begging.

'No . . . you are a mere donor . . . now get lost' . . .

From that day onwards, they come in my dreams . . . 'Father . . . Father . . . Father.'

'What kind of father? Someone, yet to see the kids . . . their mother' . . . tears were rolling down from his eyes . . .

'Doc . . . How can I console you?' I told in a sad tone. 'You better get married to Neelima . . . your hospital owner's daughter'

'Premji . . . what are you saying? You want to put me in troubles?'

'No . . . Doc . . . She is madly in love with you'

'How do you know that?'

'See Doc . . . You are a father . . . But I am a writer!'

He started laughing again . . .

June 29, 2011

15

Child Is The Father Of Man

Transfers are real headaches for all employees, irrespective of where they work . . . in government or private sector. What all new expenses, my God! From finding a good, affordable house, to a School for children . . . My best pal Sabu helped me in finding out both. Later, Father Nicholas gave me 'handwritten' receipt for rupees sixty thousand as donations, for my two children in that prestigious School.

'My provident fund is almost empty now,'I told Sabu.

'Don't blame him . . . For quality education, you have to pay,'he said while laughing

'What quality, man? An 'A' is an 'A' even in Greece . . . everything is one and the same.'

'No . . . It is quite different here, Premji . . . Management pays their teachers as per government pay scale. Whenever there is an increase in dearness allowance, Father Nicholas will send you another letter informing the increase in School fees . . . So, naturally the teachers give their best support'

'Another hike! . . . my God!'

'Only Christians know how to run good schools . . . Premji, they are dedicated people . . . You know . . . that's why even prominent Hindu politicians also let their children study here.'

'That's great . . . Unity in diversity . . . !' I laughed.

♥

Mrs&Mr;.Ramnath are my next door neighbors and they live in a palatial building of their own. He is a high profile IAS officer (Indian Administrative Service), a superb writer and wonderful man. Mrs. Ramnath is the only daughter of a multimillionaire and naturally a snob herself, due to lack of proper education. Meera is their only daughter who is a very attractive, little stout, bright girl. She is more attached to her Dad, may be due to his down to earth approach . . . no . . . beyond all he loves her the most . . . Meera and Abhi, my elder son are classmates

I used to collect our children, back from School, in my old Maruti car. Sometimes, when Mr. Ramnath was away on official tours or Mrs. Ramnath was busy with her beauty care, Meera used to join us in the evenings. But, Meera never used to invite my sons to get into her car when I couldn't reach there in time in the evenings.

'Uncle . . . How come you are so late?, she asked without any humbleness.

'My car is a pensioner . . . Meera,' I told.

'Better buy a new one.'

'I am not all rich as your Grand Pa'

'Grand Pa . . . whose Grand Pa . . . who wants his money?'there was contempt in her voice.

♥

Everything was going fairly well until the quarterly examination results got published. Meera used to adjust the first rank from first standard onwards. Fortunately or unfortunately, my elder son Abhi was declared as the class topper. It was the biggest shock of her life and of course, her mother's too! Mr. Ramnath congratulated him wholeheartedly in front of Meera and Mrs. Ramnath tried to avoid every contact my family! Poor man . . . Mr. Ramnath had to use all his administrative powers to find out some new tuition teachers and Mrs. Ramnath was overseeing everything like a ruthless supervisor of old slave farms in America!

♥

After two days, our telephone started ringing somewhere around ten'o clock in the night. Late calls in the night are symbols of danger . . . terror . . . bad news . . . I picked up the phone.

'Hello'

'Hi Uncle, Meera here . . . Can I speak to Abhi? I have to clear some doubts'

'Sure . . . one minute . . . Abhi . . . a Call for you.'

He kept the phone after sometime.

'What did she say?, my wife asked him.

'Nothing Mom . . . She was asking like . . . 'did you study this . . . did you study that . . . then . . . it is already 10PM . . . why don't you go to sleep?' . . . and you know her advice . . . 'If you don't sleep early, you cannot concentrate in class' . . . strange girl . . .'

'Idiot . . . She told you to sleep early . . . You know . . . what will she do?'

'What will she do?'

'She will learn till 12'O clock . . . Poor boy . . . he is yet to understand a girl!'

'None can understand a woman!' I teased her.

♥

That day, I had to travel to Kochi for an official training program and to my surprise Mr. Ramnath was my co-passenger. He started talking about his literary life and real life. And at last the discussions reached the saturation point: the studies of his daughter.

'Premji . . . I am not getting enough time to spend with my daughter because of her stupid tuitions.'

'I am sorry . . . Sir'

'Why do you say Sorry? You must be proud of him,' he said calmly

♥

Days went on . . . And one day, Meera was returning home with us. I stopped the car in front of an Ice-Cream parlor. My sons jumped out in uncontrollable joy as it was the first occasion in their life, eating an Ice-cream form outside! Meera was sitting there in the car itself.

'Meera, please come with us,' Abhi requested.

'No . . . Abhi . . . I don't like ice-creams . . . They contain Gelatin, made from hoof of dead animals,' she said while rejecting his plea.

'That's an interesting piece of information . . . Anyway . . . Please join us . . . At least for a company,' I told and she she followed us . . . 'That's a good move . . . listening to elders,' I told her while getting into the parlor.

'I want Butter scotch,' my younger son shouted . . .

'I like to have Vanilla,' Abhi said . . .

Waiter returned with Ice-Creams and boys started eating in big scoops thinking: 'Dad . . . today, we are going to drain out your pocket!'

'Uncle . . . why don't you have something?'Meera asked.

'Because, you are not having anything.'

'Waiter, give me one Strawberry . . . One for Uncle too,' she shouted . . .

'One for me too,'my younger son too joined her!

The children had a nice time there. I felt the radiance of happiness on their faces.

'Kids, this is the spirit of sharing and caring,' I said.

'It's really interesting, Uncle,' Meera told.

'Then why don't you avoid your tuition teachers? You and Abhi, just share your knowledge each other, then you will become the best students in Kerala State! Do you know that? How much time can you save?'

'That seems interesting,' Abhi and Meera, they told together.

'Then you can teach him too,' I showed them my younger son. 'Meera, not even a single time in life, you father had taken any tuitions! And he has achieved the finest post position an individual can achieve in this nation . . . Indian Administrative Service . . . Keep that always in mind . . . You know he is missing you a lot because of your tuitions'

'Uncle . . . how do you know all these?'

'He told me'. She kept quiet. 'Meera, how many Ice-Creams do you eat everyday?'

'Three or four'

'That's why you are getting stout . . . reduce the numbers . . . check the ill-effects of Ice-creams in the internet . . . Never forget this Meera . . . your Dad used to study under lamp posts, even during rain . . . He was not rich enough . . . Have you ever seen him wasting a single paisa for luxuries?'

'No'

'That is called thriftiness . . . Meera . . . you have the best role model ever in your home itself . . . Your Dad . . . He is a living example of hard work.'

'Yes . . . Uncle . . . I love him . . . Respect him . . . I follow his footsteps,'clouds of tears were forming in her eyes.

'The purpose of education is not good grades . . . or getting a good job . . . it's beyond all these . . . it's a highway to a better individual . . . a refined human being! Competition should be there, only healthy competition . . . Beyond every competition, there is humanity . . . Meera.'

'Thanks . . . Uncle . . . you have opened my eyes,' Meera wiped her tears.

'Not me . . . Your Dad!'

'Thanks Dad' . . . They all said together . . .

'From tomorrow onwards, we all will travel by our School Bus. What do you say, Uncle?' Meera asked.

'That's a great development . . . go forward . . .'

'Hooooooooo . . . Done,'they laughed.

♥

Ramanth had to cut every Tuition Master, though his wife was shouting like anything. Meera was very happy that day as could spent a lot of time with her father. She asked him a lot of questions so that she can share her additional knowledge with Abhi. He inspired her quest for more and more knowledge. She used to spend a lot of time with Abhi. Naturally my wife was suspicious.

'Will anything go wrong between them?'she asked.

'You were behind me even from School days . . . Did anything go wrong?'

'Nothing . . . But times are changing,'some elements of anxiety was there in her voice.

'India is emerging very fast . . . God knows . . . will there be marriages after ten years?'we laughed

♥

Meera was busy reading 'Stigma,' the new poetry collection by her Dad. She loved the fresh smell of that book like the freshness of those poems. Beyond that, the book cover was one of her paintings. 'If you commit a mistake in selecting the right soul mate . . . your life will be nothing but another hell' . . . She underlined that line with a rose pencil and slept off while reading. And she woke up little late next day.

'Ktnin . . .'

Mrs. Ramnath ran towards Meera's room. She was shocked to see her daughter shivering with anger, with that 'Stigma' in her left hand. The large mirror fixed on the cupboard was missing . . . Broken glass pieces were scattered all over the room.

'Meera . . . Have you gone mad?'she shouted . . .

'Get lost . . . you lousy ass.'

'Whatdid you call me?'

'Bloody hell . . . get lost from my room.'

'What the hell did I do to hurt you to shout on me like this?'

'What is this? See what have you done to this book?'

'What have I done?'

'What have I done? You . . . you had used . . . the first copy of my Dad's book to cover that large tumbler with steaming milk . . . See every page is wet . . . You spoiled it and talking shamelessly'

'Who cares your Dad's stupidities?'

'Stupid, illiterate, rich woman like you, doesn't care the merits of her husband . . . How can a donkey understand that world is not flat! The social status you enjoy everyday is the reward of his stupidities . . . Not of your Dad's filthy money, accumulated through corruption . . .'

'Youuu . . .'

'Get lost from my sight . . . Wait . . . I will not talk to you any more in my life,' Meera shouted aloud and started crying . . .

Her mother walked away quite confused . . .

♥

Meera and her parents visited my house to attend our younger son's birthday after one month.

'Congrats Meera . . . I am going to recommend your parents for the best couple award of the year!' I told her while serving her another cup of Ice-cream.

July 17, 2011

16

Scent Of A Woman

THAT SMALL LAKE AND the Sea were separated by a thin band of sand. And I used to stand here, on the long bridge above the lake, to watch Sun set in my younger days. And that day, I stood there again . . . But, with a difference: I was in Uniform, Circle Inspector of Police. The dead-body of a very young woman was floating over lake water . . . Was it a suicide or a murder? God knows . . . It's the head ache of every Policeman . . .

'Sir, he had gone somewhere . . . mobile is also switched off,' the Policemen who went in search of Thampi, former cadaver keeper in the Medical College, said.

'It's already getting late . . . How can we lift her body from water before nightfall?'I asked the crowd whose eyes were busy moving along with her floating body . . . 'Can anyone help us?'

They didn't reply either yes or no . . . numbskulls . . . I was in a huge dilemma . . . Then somebody stopped a modified Mahindra Scorpio SUV near me.

'Hi . . . Premji'

'Hi . . . Nazar . . . When did you come from London?'

'Three days back . . . I thought of meeting you . . . with Royal Salute,' he laughed . . . 'Tell me, what's going on here?'

'Dead body of a young woman is floating down . . . and nobody is ready to lift her up,' I spelled out my desperation.

'Is that a real problem?'Nazar asked.

'Yes'

He parked the vehicle on a side and started removing his shoes.

'What are you up to?'

'Just to lift her up,' he smiled while removing his jeans and shirt. 'Just two minutes,' he jumped into the Scorpio SUV. He consumed nearly 200 ml of raw Vat 69. 'Just for some guts,' he laughed.

'Thudd.' He plunged into the water and within no time she was lying on the ground. She was about to swell and her eyes were eaten by fishes . . . The public were busy raping her with their eyes.

'To lift a dead body in your place, someone has to come from UK . . . Now . . . Get lost you . . . Bastards,'I shouted burning with anger . . . 'Dirty sons of bitches . . .'

Nazar laughed while consuming the remaining Vat 69.

♥

After two weeks, he called from UK and I envisioned what happened in his house there in UK . . . through his words . . .

My son was away at school . . . and only my wife was there at home. When I was to hug her, she pushed me away. Did she smell something foul on my body?

'Is this the way to treat your husband when he is back after a long journey?'

'Of course . . . it is like this . . . Mr. Nazar . . . Answer me . . . why did you lift her dead body?'

'Dead body? Whose dead body?'

'Don't try to act . . . Mummy rang up and told me'

'Did your Mom get training from Scotland Yard?'

'Naaaazar . . . don't try to change the subject . . . God knows . . . whether she was a prostitute or an AIDS patient . . . tell me . . . Why did you lift her body?'

'You want to know that?'

'Yes . . . I must'

'Whether dead or alive . . . women deserve respect,' I said calmly and she hugged me tight in a quick move . . .

'Scent of a woman! I feel the scent of a woman on your body,' she said calmly . . .

July 15, 2011

17

Destined To Win

Kochi . . . People call her 'The Queen of Arabian Sea' and a part of my life belongs to her. During my vibrant youth, I was working for a corporate firm in Kochi, dealing with all kind of Automobiles. I had to sell all types of capital equipment, for a living, with a price tag starting from rupees one million to hundred millions! Imagine, just one man to manage the entire sales in Kerala and that too he had to achieve the target! Otherwise, incentives would remain as a dream! What a hectic life!

I was staying in a lodge, that too in the heart of Kochi, with so many dignified drunkards and I used to go home only once in a month, even though the distance is less than two hundred kilometers. On one Sunday, we were watching a live Cricket match on Television . . . A match between India and Pakistan and tension among spectators were growing up in geometric progression per every ball! Suddenly, Saji announced sad news.

'Princess Diana is no more'

'How do you know that?' I asked.

'From BBC . . . Princess and her boyfriend Dodi-al-Fiad . . . they both got killed in a fatal accident . . . somewhere in France'

'Sure . . . it could be a well-planned murder,' I told my opinion . . . 'a secret plot'

'May be,' Sethuvettan announced his support for my argument.

'Were she pregnant?'Saji asked.

'God knows.'

'Her numbers were totally against her. Unlucky 12 . . . and she was victimized,' I told.

The arguments heated up, Cricket too . . . O.'a lightening four' by Yuvraj Singh . . . We won the match . . . it was a day of great loss for the world and great victory for India. Suddenly telephone started ringing and Saji ran to his room.

'Please don't do that . . . please don't commit suicide . . . your life is so precious . . . you have no right to kill it,' same stereotype dialogues of a counselor; Saji was desperately trying to save a life . . . Always, I respected his integrity.

I used to help him to stick posters in public places and place stickers in transport buses during free time. He was a member of some Charismatic group and had been running a twenty four hour free counseling center for years. We friends helped him to manage it without any break. Saji was such a nice guy that he was not having any bad habits . . .

'Smoking, drinking and masturbation . . . I will not commit all these sins during my life,' he told me once.

'Better, you commit suicide! Idiot . . . a life, not worth living!' I laughed aloud.

♥

That day, we had an official party . . . Expensive liquor was flooding in the party! A Keralite will drink even acid, if it is given for 'free'! I was totally out of senses when someone dropped me back! I slept off immediately, not even aware of the cloud of mosquitoes which were ready to lift and leave me on 'her' lap! My sweet . . . !

Somebody knocked on my door at around midnight. I wanted to kill that bastard . . . just one unexpected stab will be enough to . . .

'Who the fuck is that?'

'It's me . . . Saji'

'You . . . senseless bastard . . . What the hell do you want?'

'Premji . . . Just open the door . . . man . . .,' he kept on knocking.

Rusty hinges . . . The door creaked, just like my mind, while opening. Saji was standing there in the darkness, only his teeth were visible . . .

'You . . . soul of darkness . . . What do you want?'

'Lock the door and come with me.'

I followed him to his room. Suddenly he started wearing fresh clothes . . .

'Where the hell are you going?'

'Now, listen Premji . . . My girlfriend's brother . . . he had met with an accident . . . Drunken driving . . . He is the only earning member of her family . . . careless idiot.'

'Every idiot has a girlfriend! Calling a drunkard 'an idiot' is a sin . . . Indirectly, you are calling me an idiot! You . . . 'tea-bag' . . . how can you understand the pleasure of drinking?'

'O . . . please don't eat my brains.'

'So, you want my blood?'

'No, Man . . . If I take you for blood donation, you know, what will they say? 'There is only meager amount of blood in 'alcohol' . . . and that too inseparable, even by God!' we laughed.

'Good assessment! Now, what should I do?'I was feeling more and more sleepy.

'Give me your Bike key . . . and tonight you are sleeping here . . . If anyone calls, please attend'

'OK. Done . . . if I vomit here?

'You can clean that in the morning,' he vanished in the dark.

'Your Dad will clean.'

♥

I thought of removing the receiver from the cradle so that I could get some sleep without any interference . . . But, who prevented me from doing that?

I slept off again. When the telephone started ringing frantically, I was floating over a dream . . . acting as hero in a love song with my office receptionist . . . We were not at all in good terms as we had a fight earlier! I was not at all interested to blow up her ego . . .

'O! God! Which bastard is that? Not even allowing me to enjoy an impossible dream,'I started grunting while getting up.

'Hello,' my voice was not clear . . .

'Hello . . . Is it 'flame of hope' counseling center?' (Flame . . . what a name for a counseling center!)

'Yes, May I help you?'

'No . . . I got your number from a local bus'

'So? What is your problem?'I was getting irritated.

'I am going to commit suicide,' he told in a tired voice. 'right now'

'Brother . . . You decision is wrong . . . Life is the gift of God, and you have no right to kill it,' I started counseling him like a parrot, that too in drunken voice.

'I have taken the right decision . . . I will die within ten minutes . . . Cyanide is ready . . . Now, I will not listen to anybody's advice,' he started laughing. Idiot . . . spoiled my dearest dream . . .

'You, son of a bitch . . . go and get fucked up somewhere in the hell,' I slammed the phone, raging with anger . . . A drunken night had become sinking night . . . 'Saji, I will show you my charisma, if you won't get me another full bottle tomorrow . . .'

Within five minutes, telephone started ringing again.

'Hello,' he was on the line.

'Bastard . . . Are you still alive?'

'I have dropped the plan to kill myself.'

'Why? Bastards like you are burden to any family . . . And to the Earth also . . . Better revoke your decision'

'When a stupid counselor like you, doesn't even value my precious life, why should I commit suicide? I know how to lead a life of honour . . . Understand Mr. Counselor.'

'Counselor? Who is your counselor? Me? Ha . . . ha . . . Ha . . . Bastard, I am just a drunkard! Now, leave me alone and go to sleep.'

'Sorry Boss . . . I will give you a treat, tomorrow . . . You taught me a simple lesson . . .'

'What is that?'

'Man is destined to win . . . Thank You . . . Good night Boss . . . ,' he laughed from the other end.

July 11, 2011

18

Caliph And The Maid

Baghdad . . . long back, it was the city of gardens, riches and peace. The reign of Caliph Harun al Rashid Rashid, they say, it was the golden times of Iraq . . .

A beautiful maid was recruited for housekeeping in the Royal Palace. She was from a very poor family and her only asset was her stunning beauty. She knew that better than anyone.

One day, around noon, she entered into the King's chamber. For the first time in her life, she watched the most expensive things in the world. Deep in her mind, she made a quick comparison between the King and her. 'Sad, I am just a broom stick,' she sighed and started cleaning everything. At last, she was busy replacing the silk bed covers.

'O! God! How smooth is this bed!'

That bed was made up of the feathers of Royal Swans. She had an uncontrollable wish . . . just to lie on that . . . Poor girl looked around . . . O, none were there in the vicinity.

♥

The Caliph, returned, very tired, after a long session in the court, was shocked to see his maid in deep slumber, that too on his expensive royal bed. He slapped on her face in uncontrollable anger. She cried aloud in pain . . . Her red cheek started swelling . . . She then started laughing madly . . . uncontrollably . . .

'Strange woman' . . . the King thought . . . 'Crying and laughing'

'Why did you laugh? If you don't answer, I will cut your throat right now,' he pulled out the blood thirsty sword.

'Pardon me . . . Your Majesty . . . You have punished me with such a slap, just for sleeping only once on this bed. Every-day you sleep in this bed . . . I couldn't control my laughter . . . just by thinking . . . how many more slaps will be reserved for you by Allah!'

Harun al Rashid left the palace on the very day and later he became a Sufi. She too accompanied him.

♥

Abdul, a boy of seventeen, was busy reading the story from the text book of a school girl sitting next to him, in that crowded bus. Somehow, he managed to stop the bus amidst that wide desert.

♥

He sat under the cool shade of a date-palm tree . . . One ripe date fell on his lap . . .

'Grace of Allah . . .

He put that date in his mouth. The timer on his belt bomb was busy running down 60 . . . 59 . . . 58 . . . 57 . . . 56 . . . 55 . . .

'You are that eternal sweetness,' the desert breeze murmured in his ears.

June 24, 2011

19

Juvenile Home

Ramu, a ten year old boy, was really fascinated by the new Apple I-phone his father uses. His curiosity grew up uncontrollably as his father never allowed him to touch it.

One day, Ramu got an opportunity to play with it, all alone at home. What all options! He tried out the content of one video on the next door girl of five years . . . Just a chocolate was more than enough! At last, her cries were stopped by a pillow on his trembling hands.

'Murder after a rape attempt . . . ,' Police said.

♥

'An innocent boy is now inside of the juvenile home . . . Father or son, who is the real rapist, Premji?' asked my wife.

July 22, 2011

20

Citizen 'Cane'

The huge buildings of that engineering college stood on steel and concrete in the University Campus. The newly constructed AutoCAD Lab was situated in an empty corner. And we, Ravi and me, took three days to install 'AutoCAD 2010,' design drafting software, in the newly allotted lot of 60 brand new computers.

On the third day evening, our department head and College Principal visited the well-arranged lab and that time I was busy surfing through the internet . . . Poetfreak . . . my madness . . . Ravi was snoring like a Spanish bull retired from fighting arena! I woke him up in a quick move without their notice.

'Premji, this is not a good habit,' HOD told jestingly . . .

'Sorry . . . Sir'

'The youth should come out of this virtual world . . . You see . . . Premji . . . University has 100 hectares of land . . . what all different types of plants, flowers, birds and butterflies . . . what all interesting things are here to watch . . . You people are not at all interested on any of them . . . very sad indeed,'our Principal said with deep anguish.

'You are right, Sir,' I said.

'You write poetry?'

'Not exactly . . . Sometimes . . . Sir'

'That's good . . . So, the software installation is over?'

'Yes . . . Sir'

'Very good,' he congratulated us. 'These guys deserve something, what shall we give them Mr. HOD?'

'Anything you like . . . Sir,' HOD had no hesitation.

'Premji . . . What do you want?'

'If you don't mind, please grant me three days off!' (Today is Wednesday, so four days with her! Oooolalalah . . .)

'Bit greedy you are . . . anyway granted,' he said.

♥

I was busy preparing my bag for leaving home when Ravi returned, that too after keeping the AutoCAD lab key in the Principal's chamber. 'Please don't torment her too much,' Ravi made fun of me . . . 'You are living like a bachelor here!'

My sons were eating my brains till late night . . . tiny monsters, were not at all sleeping! Separation makes husband and wife great lovers again and again! A mobile-ring can spoil a precious, passionate night! Passion, what a sweet and lovely word it is!

'Dear, don't wake me up till 9'O clock, tomorrow.'

'O.K . . . ,' she told while switching off the lights . . .

'Who grows the fruits of passion in darker nights?'I started singing an old melody in her ears.

'Hungry lion!' . . . She said and we ended the laughter in a tight lip-lock!

♥

'Get up please,' she made me wake up early in the morning, 'here is an urgent call for you'

'Where is my phone?'

'That's switched off . . . now please talk with Ravi'

'Bastard . . . from where did he get your number?'I collected the phone. 'Hello Ravi, is there anything really important?'

'Yes . . . Please come back before 12'O clock . . . today'

'What? Are you joking?'

'No' . . .

'O.K.'

♥

When I reached near the University campus, several Police jeeps were moving in an out.

'Kunjikka . . . Anything serious?' I enquired the watcher in the main gate.

'Sir . . . some new computers were stolen from your engineering college'

'My God!' I felt a shiver-wave on my spine.

♥

'You know . . . they didn't break the lock . . . just opened it with its own key . . . Tell me, where did you keep the key immediately after closing the lab, yesterday evening?'Rahim, the Circle Inspector asked me.

'As usual . . . Ravi kept it there in the Principal's room . . . Rahim . . . Sorry . . . Sir,'I told him without any tension because he was my classmate. 'Every key is kept there exactly on the peg with label referring to which room; it belongs to, on a big plywood board on the wall.'

'That means, Premji, they might have picked up the key from the Principal's office earlier . . . and made a duplicate . . . The original key is still hanging there on that board . . . ,' he started breaking his head analyzing the crime. 'That means that the thief is from within'

♥

The enquiry was going on in faster pace and I tried to collect maximum details of the notorious guys in the vicinity. One day, some of my colleagues were busy discussing about a new second computer shop in Kochi, where almost new computers were available at cheaper rate. I collected their address and reached there in that evening. The sales department people were very happy to deal with me and they offered the best price. I checked the machines.

And on the very next day, the most popular (notorious) gang in the University Campus were arrested by Rahim, based on the information transferred by me. They had opened a second hand Computer shop in the city just to dispose the sixty computers with the help of their friends who were in computer business! What an idea!

♥

The students . . . totally six members . . . they were standing in a row, heads down, in the Police station. Rahim and I, we were busy discussing something inside his chamber. Suddenly, he was summoned by DGP and before leaving he called the Asst. Sub-Inspector (ASI). A tough old man in uniform, nearing the age of pension, appeared there in no time. He was notorious for his skill for 'interrogation'! Wonderful muscles he had even in the fag-end of his service.

'Samuel . . . see, I have to go out now . . . You just . . . bring out the truth,' Rahim said.

'Understood Sir'

'Good,' they laughed. 'Premji . . . you can see the whole episode from here,' Rahim told me while leaving.

'OK Rahim'. When he left the chamber, I repositioned the chair.

♥

'Bastards . . . lift your heads up,' Samuel started his specialization: 'bloodless psychic surgery' with a long cane in hand. He was a notorious 'intelligent torturer' during the period of emergency in the seventies. How many youth were crushed under his boots! He started asking their whereabouts . . . all were from very rich families and at last Samuel located him, Anzil.

'Bastard . . . your father is a personal friend of mine . . . What a nice man he is . . . and you son of a bitch . . . He has money even for another five more generations . . . you steal things instead of studies . . . Bastard . . . you better kill your Dad.'

Anzil stood like rock, looking downward, without any change of expression on his face . . . no matter of repentance!

'Why did you commit a crime like this?

'Crime? I was totally helpless Sir . . . You know . . . Sir, I have a 1000 CC imported Kawasaki Ninja bike,'he opened his mouth and started talking as if nothing had happened or he was totally innocent! 'it has a very poor mileage of just 10 km/ litre . . . Dad gives just Rs. 500/— as daily allowance . . . Sir, please tell me, how can a youth like me survive on that meagre sum? Just one round inside our Campus, Rs. 500/—petrol will be over . . . Sir, I have to give treats to my girlfriends . . . Now-a-days girls are very cunning . . . Sir . . . they eat only expensive Ice-creams . . . watch movies only in multiplexes . . . even though they drink porridge at home . . . then I have drop them in their homes . . . then I have to have snacks, beer, cigarettes with my gang . . . I like to eat royally from outside . . . life is hectic Sir . . . you know it is very expensive . . . Sir, petrol is my worst enemy . . . without money, you are absolutely waste . . . Sir,' he was narrating as if he was talking with a long-time friend.

'So . . . Anzil . . . Tell me your daily expense? Samuel asked quite coolly . . . after all he is the friend of the boy's father!

'Sir, petrol expenses is of around rupees one thousand . . . maintaining my girlfriends another thousand . . . for friends another thousand . . . and another five hundred for my food and personal health-care . . . Sir, I love to spend three hours in Gym . . . I have to find out some three thousand five hundred rupees daily decent living in my college . . . Sir . . . but . . . you know . . . I go there only six or seven days in a month . . . Sir,' he kept on talking.

'So, what is your monthly expense?'

'Not up to your imagination, Sir . . . approximately some twenty five thousand . . . that's not enough . . . and other expenses extra . . . that's all,' he said, living out his tension . . .

'Pataarrrr' . . . ASI Samuel slapped on his left cheek . . . He saw almost all stars in the Universe! The first and finest slap ever in his life! Poor guy, he lost all the confidence that his father would come and save him! Jail . . . jail . . . everywhere!

'You . . . Son of a bitch . . . I have 32 years of service in Police . . . and my salary is less than half of your monthly expenses . . . You know, I can collect only ten thousand rupees as net income after all sort of deductions . . . And with those ten thousands, I meet all the expenses of . . . mine . . . my wife . . . my aged mother . . . and three grown up daughters . . . Bastard . . . and you are saying . . . twenty five thousand rupees is not enough . . . for a month,' Samuel was shouting like an enraged gladiator . . .

'Bastardszzzzzzzzzzzzzzzzzz . . . ,' the canes started hissing like Cobras . . .

July 14, 2011

21

Candle In The Wind

'The mind of a modern man is a lifelong porn serial. He is the hero of every episode and almost every woman he sees are his new heroines.' What a truthful comment, Sumangala thought while going through a comment by a prominent cultural leader. Every page of every daily tells the stories of sex abuse of poor minor girls.

Every sex maniac spends money for personal enjoyment. But, every newspaper owner mints money just by running filthy stories in pretext of news! Client and the pimp! What kind of dirty world is this? Its better abstain from reading to avoid hypertension in every morning!

'God! What is happening to me? What is irritating me just like a grain of sand trapped inside an oyster?'

'Write . . . write . . . write it out,'her inner voice commanded. She picked up her daughter's writing pad. Words started flowing like a torrent.

'Every woman has to resist the attacks against her. She has to groom herself to face any tough situation in life! The woman of seventy five years raped by her blood relative of thirty five . . . The five year old minor girl whose body was hidden inside a hole in a tree trunk . . . what resistance can they offer? So the argument on resistance is baseless'. Her pen started flying like a meteor approaching Earth with immense velocity. Go . . . hit . . . and powder everything . . .

'How to groom a woman? The world has been discussing this matter from time immemorial. It's enough . . . Let's stop all discussions . . . She doesn't need any of your suggestions . . . advises . . . Let her groom her life . . . Let her be free from chains . . .

Now, there is immense material available to corrupt our boys . . . internet, movies . . . advertisements . . . let's start discussing how to groom our boys . . . just to avoid innocent minor boys ending up in jails for attempting sex abuse.'

What a relief! Artists are the luckiest people for they only can enjoy absolute happiness . . . Bliss after the pain of creativity . . . Sumangala understood that simple fact immediately before closing her pen.

It was a lazy Sunday and I was still on bed. My wife was busy surfing in the internet for some information for a student project. Suddenly my phone started ringing.

'Suma is on the line,' my wife told while handing over the phone to me.

I switched on the loud speaker after watching the curiosity on my wife's face.

'Hello'

'Hi Premji . . . Good morning . . . Sumangala here'

'Hi Suma'

'Are you sitting in front of your laptop?'

'No. But, why?'

'I have posted my first article on facebook'

'That's interesting. One minute Suma' . . . I told her to hold the phone and collected the laptop from my wife. Immediately I located her post.

'Premji, did you go through it?'

'Yes'

'How is it?'

'Interesting thought . . . Being the father of two naughty boys, sure, I will accept your suggestion. Anyway, congratulations! Someday, you will become a wonderful writer'

'You are flattering me'

'No way'

'Premji . . . You know one thing . . . While I was writing this article, my daughter . . . she started pestering me . . . Mummy . . . Mummy, shall I go and play with the next door boys? I let her go. But, thoughts about her were ruling me while I was writing . . . You know, she is just five years . . .

Which game are they playing? Who all are there to play with?

Premji . . . you know some sort of anxiety . . . some sort of uneasiness . . . I don't know how to name it . . . See, I know every boy near my house . . . They all are well behaved, very nice boys . . . children of very reputed parents . . . still that uneasiness . . . it continued till she came back. It starts from the very moment she goes out any day.'

'Tell her, it is called 'mother syndrome' . . . the oldest of all syndromes,' my wife laughed while watching our sons, playing outside, through the window.

August 19, 2011

22

Birthday Inside An Express Train

Mondays . . . Now-a-days, I hate Mondays!

'Mom . . . Please wake me also up along with you in the morning,' my eight year old elder son pleaded last Sunday night.

'Me too . . . Mom,' my younger son too joined him.

'O.K . . . done,' she told while giving them good night kisses.

'Thanks Mom . . . Good night,' they both slept off soon.

'Premji . . . Our boys are really missing us . . . When will we both get transfer to Trivandrum again?'she asked painfully.

'Soon dear,' I consoled her. Even we had to store love for another week!

♥

Alarm, set in the mobile phone, started ringing exactly at 3 am. These machines don't have souls! Love too! She woke me up and we both got ready soon to leave for our destinations where we both work. She is staying there in college hostel where she works as an assistant professor and I am staying in an old house with my friend where I work. A family is torn into three fragments as our sons are staying with their grandma!

And one last look . . . Both the boys were sleeping peacefully and I could find a cute smile on the younger one's face.

'He is dreaming of some Tom and Jerry cartoons,' I said.

'No . . . he is dreaming of me,'she said.

We both wanted to kiss them. But, we couldn't . . . a kiss may wake them up.

'If I can see you both leaving in the morning, I won't be feeling so sad in the morning,' my elder son's words started reverberating in our ears.

♥

Somehow, we managed to get into a small van, traveling to the city regularly in the early morning, jam-packed with fishermen about to go for fishing in the dark Sea. Life is a journey for daily bread for you and me, dear brothers! But, how many of us understand this simple truth?

♥

She ran towards Thiruvananthapuram bus-stand and I transformed to another Usain Bolt to the railway station. It was sheer luck . . . I could manage to jump into the moving train . . . Venad Express . . . Lucky I was as I could save another half day casual leave! I bought some newspapers from a vendor and started turning pages to find out the reviews about our literary festival . . . Trivandrum literary festival, concluded on last Sunday. Deccan chronicle, they gave us wonderful coverage, Indian Express too . . . Within no time, I slept off like a new-born . . . The past four days, we were running like greased machines to realize our dream . . . the literary festival . . . a festival for the lesser known and of the lesser known Indian English poets!

Chenganoor Railway station . . . Who made me wake up when the train reached the penultimate train stop I had to get down? Thanks God! I cleaned my face with some sweet smelling tissue papers to wipe away the fragments of sleep.

'Good Morning, Sir,' a teenage boy sitting next to me greeted me.

'Thanks . . . Good Morning'

'Sir, will you pass on that daily?'

'Sure'

He returned it back with an innocent smile on his face within two minutes.

'He wants to talk to you,' my heart told me.

'Sir, today is my birthday,' he told while handing me over a toffee.

'Many . . . many . . . happy returns of the day . . . young man'

'Thank you . . . Sir'

'By the way, what is your name?'

'Graham . . . Sir, I am studying for Civil Engineering in Rajiv Gandhi Institute of Technology at Kottayam'

'Sounds great'

'Chechee (elder sister), today is my birthday,' he told the girl sitting immediately opposite to me while handing over a toffee. Soon he started issuing toffees to almost every passenger in that cabin.

She started crushing it between her fingers . . .

I was watching his actions with curiosity. What a lovely boy, he is! But, soon his face started darkening like a black hole . . .

Nobody . . . nobody in that compartment put those toffees in their mouths! Nobody!

'What kind of stupid world is this,' I thought while putting that pealed toffee into my mouth. 'Idiots! After all, he is a small boy . . . not at all going to steal any of your valuables, just by giving you a toffee.'

Suddenly, morning Sun rose up on his face like a blossoming Lotus!

What a smile! What an aura!

You gave the smile of my life! Toffee too!

Thanks . . . Jesus . . . Thanks . . . My human God!

♥

I stood there in the platform watching him moving away with the speeding train. I started walking light-hearted.

I picked up a crushed toffee from the empty platform and I could feel it, so heavy like those thirty silvers!

September 28, 2011

23

Silence

Being a poet, my religion is nothing but humanity. Since the year of joining government service, I used to celebrate Christmas along with my students. You know, we have ten days of official holidays for Christmas! Last Christmas . . . how can I forget the last Christmas?

♥

I was sitting all alone in staff room and some of my students approached me with very pleasing smiles on their faces.

'Good Morning . . . Sir.'

'Good Morning boys . . . Merry Christmas'

'Thank you, Sir . . . We wish you a merry Christmas and a Happy New Year'

'Thanks . . . then?'

'Sir, your share . . .'

I gave them Rs.100/—and they left happily, wishing me Happy Christmas once again. Sunil, our office peon, entered in the meantime with his two year old son.

'Hi, Chottu . . . Happy Christmas,' I welcomed the kid. But, he kept quiet.

'Chottu . . . Say 'hello' to Premji uncle,' Sunil gave him instruction and he obeyed lovingly.

'Hello Uncle . . . Good Morning'

'Good Morning Chottu . . . you are a nice boy,' I congratulated him.

'Sir, please don't entertain these boys by giving money for celebrations . . . That's fundamentally wrong . . . You know what they are telling now? 'Premji Sir gave us rupees hundred . . . why can't you give at least fifty?' Who knows whether they are going to spend this money for buying liquor?' Sunil registered his protest.

'Is that so?'

'Yes'

'Forgive them Sunil . . . after all it's Christmas'

'Uncle . . . Chocolates,' Chottu said.

'You want Chocolates?'

'No . . . No . . . please have it . . . It's my treat' . . . Chottu handed me over two Chocolates.

'Thanks Chottu . . . but for what?'

'Papa bought a new 'peepee' . . . brmm . . . brrmmm . . . ,' he started riding an imaginary bike inside the room.

'Sir, I bought a Hero Honda Splendor Bike yesterday,' Sunil said while pointing towards that bike parked outside. It looked like a cute damsel!

'Nice bike Sunil . . . So, now you are free from the daily rush in local buses . . .'

'Sir, you are capable of buying 100 bikes . . . but you don't even own a Cycle! Why?'

'It's not good for a poet! I will sit only as a pillion rider, not as a rider,' We laughed. But, Chottu couldn't understand anything.

Students started singing Carol songs downstairs.

'Papa . . . take me there,' Chottu said while pulling the hands of Sunil.

Sunil . . . what a wonderful colleague . . .

♥

Five years back . . . Sunil, unemployed then, was in silent love with Sumangala, daughter of a very close relative. But, she got married to someone who was a high ranking government servant. She had a wonderful life till that fateful day . . . exactly till their first wedding anniversary . . . Her husband had booked earlier a seat to Cochin by train. He missed the train as their family car, driven by her Dad, broke down in the middle. Somehow, her father arranged a seat for him in a luxury bus as he had to attend a very important conference.

A telephone call by POLICE woke her up in the middle of the night informing the sad demise of her husband as their bus collided with a heavy truck carrying steel. Driver slept off, it seems! Sumangala stopped talking to her father from that day. 'You killed my husband,' those were the last words she exchanged with her Dad. Women are strange beings! She tormented her Dad with absolute silence . . . I am aware of each and every move in their family as her father is a dear friend of mine.

In the meantime, Sunil joined our College as a peon and was deputed to our department. Accidentally, I came to know the reason why Sunil remained as a bachelor. I told the whole matter to my wife and she arranged for a meeting at my home. Sumangala and Sunil got married on the very next day. Poor girl wanted to run away from her rich home! I had some doubts: will she be able to live with his poor salary? My doubts were baseless . . . Love could do wonders . . .

Sunil dropped me back home in the evening.

'Sunil, please don't drop him again by bike,' my wife warned him.

'Why? Chechi.'

'I don't like him travel by bikes . . . They are the most unsafe things in this world . . . Don't take Chottu along with you on bike . . . Again . . . don't let him sit on the petrol tank.'

'Chechi, he is an expert . . . he knows how to cling on there.'

'You are an idiot . . . when will you understand the anguish of a mother?'

♥

I had a call from Dr. Ashok within half an hour. Chottu was sleeping on hospital bed with bandages all over. Sunil stood beside him, unhurt, crying.

'Chottu is alright, Premji . . . Nothing to worry,' Dr. Ashok told me.

'What happened exactly?'

'Chottu fell down when Sunil tried to avoid a tipper loaded with sand.'

'Did he vomit, Ashok?'

'I think not . . . but, he has some wounds on his face . . . Nothing to worry . . .'

'Any sort of head injury? Any need for scanning?'

'I think . . . No . . . now you take him home . . . Give him these medicines . . . If he feels any sort of pain, bring him here tomorrow morning . . .'

I took Chottu back home in a Taxi and Sunil followed us closely on his bike. Poor guy was tensed so much . . . how to face Sumaangala? I promised his earlier that I would manage the situation . . . But? Sumangala stopped talking with Sunil when she saw the bandages on her son's body

♥

'Om . . . Gam Ganapataye Nama: . . . Om . . . Gam Ganapataye Nama:'My new ringtone woke me up around eight'o clock in the morning. Who the hell is that . . . not at all allowing me to sleep peacefully even on a holiday?

'Sir . . . is Sunil there?'Sumangala was on the other end.

Where the hell is my underwear? Who needs it when you wear dirty jeans! I stood there in front of her house within ten minutes. Lucky I was . . . I didn't faint inhaling the foul smell came out from my own mouth . . . I didn't even wash my face.

'How is Chottu?'

'He is alright . . . he woke up bit late in the morning . . . again went back to sleep after having some milk . . . You know . . . Sunil left home at around five'o clock in the morning' Suma had some tension.

'Didn't he tell you where he was going?'

'No . . . I didn't ask'

'O! You are observing silence! Suma, this is not fair . . . Did you try him over phone at least?'

'No'

'O.K . . . Let me call him'. But, his mobile was switched off. 'Did you have a fight in the morning?'

'No'

'Then, for God's sake . . . tell me what all happened yesterday?'

'I was crying almost all night . . . and unknowingly I slept off in the middle . . . Sunil was sitting near Chottu; wake up, all night . . .'

'Then?'

'There was a Voltage drop early in the morning . . . I woke up seeing him trying to wake the boy up in dim light. Chottu didn't open his eyes . . . He was in deep sleep, may be due to sedation of the medicine . . . Sunil then went out on his bike . . . May be to meet someone.'

I tried to locate him by calling all his friends . . . Obliviously; all are my friends too . . . None knew where he was. At last, I called him, Johny: our college watcher.

'Sir, he is sitting there in the poen's rest room.'

'Where are you now?'

'I am at home'

'O.K. Johny,' I cut the call. 'Don't worry Suma . . . He is there in our college.'

♥

His red Splendor bike was parked in the two wheeler shed. I walked towards the rest room. But, I was stopped by some yellow liquid flowing out from the closed room . . . still hot . . . what the hell is that? And the door is locked from inside . . . I could feel darkness encircling my eyes . . . I broke the door . . . Who imparted me strength to break those teak planks?

Head stooping down, he was hanging on the ceiling fan . . . What were his bulging eyes wanted to tell me? I unfolded a piece of paper, got from his wet pocket.

'Forgive me Suma . . . I killed my son . . . I cannot live without him . . . I cannot face you anymore . . . Sorry . . . I too follow him to eternal silence . . . I love you . . . Painfully yours . . . Sunil' . . .

September 09, 2011

24

Akeldama

Gautama stood near the corpse of Judas Iscariot. Hot blood was still gushing out from his broken skull. The potter's field remained like a red painting made of blood and his bowels, gushed out, looked like mating pythons.

'One-day, this place will be known as 'the field of blood'; Gautama told himself and sank into deep meditation. When he opened his eyes, Jesus was sitting beside him in tears . . .

'Why do you cry?'

'Sacrifice recognizes sacrifice.' replied Jesus.

Buddha smiled and that smile got transferred to Jesus also, for true smile is made of sacrifice!

October 12, 2011

25

Indian English!

'Premji . . . are you there in Trivandrum?' Maya inquired through mobile phone.

'Yes . . . I am here in the city . . . What's the matter?'

'Please come down to Kerala House . . . We have to discuss something very important'

'O.K . . . Done . . . I will be there in twenty minutes . . . bye'

♥

She was waiting outside beside her Kinetic Honda Scooter. How many summers and winters, the scooter looked like a collage made of mud! We went inside of that restaurant and sat in a lone corner.

'Tea'

'Sorry Madam . . . its lunch time,' bearer informed politely.

'It's already 2.30 pm'

'That doesn't matter Madam'

'O.K. Then . . . Get us two pineapple juice,' I said calmly.

'Please have this Madam,' the waiter returned back within a moment, with two cups of Payasam (sweets)

'Is it free?'

'Yes Madam . . . It takes some time to prepare the juice'

'Thanks then' . . . Maya smiled.

He walked away.

'Maya . . . Now, tell me the matter'

'Premji . . . 16th May is nearing . . . the first anniversary of our literary journal . . . We should celebrate that in a different way . . . What do you say?'

'I agree with you completely'

'What about a literary festival?'

'That sounds great!'

'O.K. Then . . . decided'

'Funds?'

'Where there is a will, there is a way!'

'God bless all of us!'

She made some immediate calls and within ten minutes six of our friends arrived. Lucky we were, by that time the pineapple juices were over!

'Sir, anything more?' waiter asked

'Eight cups of tea'

'Sir, it will take a minimum of half an hour'

'No problem . . . You can take your own time,' I laughed.

Kerala House is the only place in the city where we can meet and talk without much expenditure!

'Maya . . . Have you seen this?' Jacob took out an invitation . . . 'Writer Sunita Gopal will be there in Modern Books today . . . form 4.30 pm . . . A book reading cession . . . followed by an open forum . . . Are you coming?'

'Sure . . . If possible, we can take an interview also so that we can publish it next month,'

And our discussions went on up to 4.25 pm.

'O.K . . . The literary festival for Indian English Writers is decided to be conducted on . . . ,' Maya announced.

'That usage itself is incorrect . . . It should be corrected like this 'Indians writers who write in English,' old man Jos Mathew presented his suggestion.

'No way . . . We write in Indian English only! Those who write like Americans or Britishers are considered as Indian

English writers! We can't accept that!' we all supported her argument.

♥

We all met again on the very next week . . . Same place . . . Kerala House . . . Long live the manager!

'I met KNB and we had a small discussion . . . Readily, he agreed to be our chief patron . . . What an exceptional writer and a wonderful man! Three times Literary Academy award winner!' Maya told us with lot of enthusiasm!

'We have decided almost everything except the most important thing,' I said.

'What's that?'

'Funds!'

'I don't think that will be a huge problem . . . Hay festival was over very recently . . . they had enough sponsorship . . . We will also get,' Jos Mathew was thoroughly optimistic.

'They have enough sponsorship from Publishers, unlike us . . . Hay festival is launched in India targeting at high income IT employees . . . They buy books to get out of the monotony of job . . . Its pure business my friend . . . We are 'out of that business,' I told my frank opinion.

'Everything is O.K . . . Venue is the same . . . Kanakakunnu Palace,' Jacob said.

♥

'Premji,' Maya called again after two weeks. 'We are in trouble'

'Why?'

'KNB won't be able to attend our event . . . You know . . . poor man is too busy as he is awarded with Gyanpith, the highest literary honour of our nation . . . Premji . . . We have to find someone, eminent, to inaugurate the festival'

'Next alternative?'

'I have contacted Sunita Gopal,'

'Who is she?'

'Don't you know her? She is the new princess of Indian writers who write in English . . . She wrote some five novels . . . all are best sellers . . . got translated into more than 20 languages . . . You know . . . that day I collected her phone number,'

'Then, what did she say?'

'She is ready to come from Hyderabad . . . But, we have to bear the air tickets . . . She will come in the morning flight and leave by the evening'

'That's reasonable'

'Her presence will bring some colour to the inaugural cession . . . News coverage is an additional bonus . . . I told her about our economic condition . . . She agreed to fly in economic class . . . After-all she is a writer! She can understand much better!'

'Thanks God!'

♥

Together, we all went and met so many publishers, hoteliers, CEO's of companies at Techno-park . . . But, everyone deserted us. Who cares Indian English!

'Anyway . . . we have announced it . . . and to realize it, we have to empty our pockets,' someone told.

'Rs1,00,000/- . . . We will share it'

Suddenly Maya's mobile made some noise . . . She showed us the latest message in the in-box.

'Maya . . . What about my stay? Usually, I stay at Taj Viventa* when I am away from Hyderabad—Sunita Gopal'

'Bloody bitch!' Jos Mathew, the old man, couldn't control his anger. 'She is the Indian writer who writes in English! Bloody pen-pusher who wrote 'the story of a scavenger woman tuned prostitute' while sitting inside a five star suite!'

'What are you going to do now?' I asked her.

'Dear Madam . . . We will arrange food and accommodation at Mascot Hotel, which is very near to the venue. We are not in a position to cater your suggestion—Taj Viventa—Maya,' she showed me the freshly typed message. And within no time, it vanished in air.

♥

Sunita Gopal came in time and inaugurated the function by delivering a two minute talk. Everyone was thoroughly disappointed. The match sticks were still under fumes, lying on the ground!

'We had to waste a lot of money just for a silly 'talk' . . . Maya . . . What's happening around us?' I was getting angry.

'It seems . . . she was not aware . . . that she should deliver an inaugural address . . . We didn't inform her, it seems,'

'Superb argument! Next year, we better invite a beggar from East Fort Junction . . . What do you say?'

'Done . . . Premji . . . That will be far . . . far better! And you know one more thing,'

'What?'

'She is not going to check in to Mascot Hotel,'

'Why?'

'She has changed her plans it seems . . . She is going to visit her aunt who is staying nearby! Another five thousand rupees is gone!'

'Bloody Indian English!'

Taj Viventa*—One of the most expensive hotels in India.

November 30, 2011

26

Life Skills

'Premji . . . Tell me . . . your frank opinion about your Sony HD handy-cam,' Dr. Prashanth, my psychologist friend, requested through mobile phone.

'Superb video clarity . . . Do you plan to by one?'

'No . . . no . . . Be ready with that, by 2 pm . . . Today.'

'I am not free today . . . You know . . . its November . . . All of my casual leaves are over'

'No more explanations please . . . I will come to pick you up,' he cut the phone.

Friends are real traps sometimes!

♥

Dr. Prashanth parked his brand new Toyota Innova at a lone corner of that expensive private management school and we walked straight into the Principal's chamber.

'Good afternoon Sir,' Prashanth greeted him pleasantly.

'Good afternoon Doctor . . . Please take your seat'

'Thank you . . . This is Premji . . . O.K . . . Let's get into the matter'

(I am just a spectator here!)

'See Doctor . . . I am quite new to this institution . . . We have a boy named Sameer Mohan, studying in ninth standard . . . He is a real headache for everyone . . . The whole staff wants him to be dismissed . . . His class teacher Ms. Sheela Devi threatens me . . . if I won't dismiss him, she will submit her resignation . . . But,'

'But?'

'But . . . I am against his dismissal . . . It may spoil the reputation of our school . . . You better counsel him once . . . We will decide later . . .'

♥

We selected an air-conditioned room for counseling and I kept the handy-cam hidden among the long books in the shelf in video capture mode.

'When this rubbish is over, just make a missed call,' I told while getting out.

'What did you say?'

'Rubbish'

'Idiot . . . Get out,' he laughed.

'Wind up as early as possible . . .'

♥

Sameer Mohan entered into the counseling room with his parents and his most hated rival, his class teacher, Ms. Sheela Devi. He was a tall, handsome boy around 14. The elders sat on the front row and Sameer sat in the rear.

'Sameer Mohan, are you comfortable?'

'Yes Doctor'

'Now . . . Tell me . . . What is your problem?'

'I don't have any problem'

'That's a common answer . . . See . . . I am here to counsel you . . . why? You know, very well, that everyone in this school has complaints against you'

'That's not my problem . . . Even I can simply raise a complaint against you . . . Can you do anything?'

Doctor Prashanth was shell shocked for a moment.

'See Doctor . . . This is his problem . . . He doesn't care anyone,' his mother interrupted in the middle.

'Madam . . . What are you doing?'

'Doctor . . . I am Dr. Maya Mohan, associate professor at Government Medical College'

'O.K. Madam . . . then, you might know more about child psychology?'

'Whatever written in psychology books may not be applicable sometimes in day-to-day life'

'Do you teach your son?'

'How is that possible Doctor . . . I have private practice till 10 pm everyday . . . I am a known Neurologist . . . My husband is free by around 4pm . . . But, we have arranged the best teachers for giving him tuitions,'

'Why doesn'the teach him?'

'See Doctor . . . My husband is having a PhD in Quantum Mechanics . . . He doesn't like to come down to the level of Sameer'

'Don't talk rubbish,' Mr. Mohan, her husband interrupted. 'Do you want to insult me?'

'I don't . . . But, I told the truth,' she said burning with anger . . .

'Sir . . . This is my problem . . . My parents are my real problem . . . They don't throw away their positions and knowledge in their workplaces . . . ,' Sameer declared his stand. 'What do you call this—professional jealousy?'

♥

'Ms. Sheela Devi . . . why are you so adamant on dismissing Sameer?'

'Doctor . . . He doesn't have manners . . . He never listens to anybody . . . He doesn't even allow his classmates to learn happily . . . He is a real trouble maker,'

'Do you think that he can't be corrected?'

'No way'

'In that case, who is the failure? Either you or he?'

'I can't answer it . . . I cannot tolerate a student, who does deliberate copying during examinations,' her face turned red.

'Excuse me . . . Doctor,' Sameer broke his silence. 'Even, I cannot tolerate a teacher who is a role-model for copying!'

'What do you mean Sameer?'

'Sir, she cannot even derive a simple equation or solve a silly problem without referring to either notes or textbook . . . How can I respect a teacher like her? She has no knowledge . . . only degrees she has . . . She has nothing to inspire me as a student'

Ms. Sheela Devi sat there so pale like the fallen leaves ofautumn . . . about to fall . . . struck by lightning!

'I don't care anybody who is not a friend of mine . . . parents . . . teachers . . . or anyone . . . Why should I waste time for strangers?'

'You . . . ,' Mrs. Maya Mohan was about to slap him, but, doctor didn't allow her.

'Today . . . you can hit me . . . But, one day, I can throw you to an old age home too,' Sameer told out of anger. 'If she doesn't have time to care for me, why should I care for her?'

'O.K . . . Enough . . . enough . . . Please calm down Sameer . . . calm down everyone . . . Just relax,' Dr. Prashanth said loudly . . . Suddenly office boy entered in with hot coffee . . . 'You came in the right time'

♥

'Right . . . I hope everyone is relaxed now . . . So the 'know me' session is over . . . Do you know the difference between 'I' and 'Me'? O.K . . . Let me explain . . . 'I' means . . . what I know about myself . . . and 'Me' is what you know about myself . . . So what is 'know me?' It is nothing but 'I' + 'Me' . . . So, to understand yourself more and more, you should disclose more and more about you and get feedback about you from others who know you . . . It is through asking and telling that our open pane is expanded and that we gain access to the potential within us represented by the unknown pane. As you all know the plus and minus of yours, it's time to move on to concrete decisions,' Dr. Prashanth said calmly.

'Doctor . . . I am going to stop my private practice since my son is the most valued one in our life,' Dr. Maya Mohan stood up from her chair and moved towards Sameer.

'I am going to cut all of his tuition teachers . . . We can handle any of his subjects till he reaches his degree classes . . . We don't teach him anything . . . We will just enjoy life,' Mr. Mohan said with lot of happiness . . .

'I am sorry Sameer . . . You have opened my eyes . . . I will not touch text books anymore,' Ms. Sheela Devi apologized with tears.

'Madam . . . Are you going to trouble me again?' Sameer asked innocently and Sheela started laughing loudly.

'No . . . Sameer . . . I am capable of teaching anything straight from my mind . . . So that you can also write any examination without copying . . . is that right?'

'Great . . . Thanks Mam'

'See . . . Students are like taps . . . Parents and teachers are like overhead tanks . . . If water doesn't run properly, it is not the fault of the tap . . . just clean up the tanks . . . that you can only do . . . then everything will be alright . . . ,' Dr. Prashanth told while searching through the mobile call list.

Everyone was silent for a minute. The very purpose of life is pursuit of happiness!

'Then, what about you Mr. Sameer Mohan?'

'What about him? He has already been corrected!' I said while entering into the room.

'O.K. Then . . . Thank you all,'

'Thanks Doctor . . .'

♥

I walked near the cupboard when Sameer and parents were about to walk away.

'Premji, let that be there for five more minutes,' Ms. Sheela Devi said. 'Excuse me Sir, Excuse me Madam . . . Please stay here for five more minutes'

'O.K. Madam,' they sat back again.

'Dr. Prashanth . . . I wish . . . if you could have peeled, at least, a big onion . . . or scraped half coconut in the kitchen . . . or you could have helped the kids in their studies . . . then, I wouldn't have been insulted like this today, my dear husband . . . ,' Ms. Sheela Devi ended her stubborn words.

'With all of your permission, I am going to upload this video on youtube,' I said. 'What do you say Dr. Prashanth?'

'That's the need of the hour,' he told while laughing aloud.

November 29, 2011

27

Raw Youth

It was around eight'o clock in the morning and I was standing at the bus stop near the newly constructed house of Jayesh. At last, his head appeared at a distance and I started walking toward him.

Pundits were chanting Sanskrit Mantras, sitting near the sacred fire and the house warming function was going on quite well. Friends and relatives were busy moving in and around the newly constructed house and children were playing Cricket in the courtyard. They never fail to utilize every opportunity to play even in light drizzle!

Jayesh took me inside and started showing each and every facility incorporated, proudly. Suddenly, my eyes were stopped by a wonderful painting hung on his study room.

'Jayesh, did he allow you to take a canvas print of his painting?' I asked.

'This is not a print . . . original . . . man . . . this is original,'

'Impossible,' I couldn't believe my ears . . .

'Premji . . . Saju came here yesterday evening, and presented me this . . . You know . . . he was so happy yesterday . . . You will also get one . . . he told me . . .'

♥

Saju was busy packing his paintings using huge brown papers when I reached his home. His personal gallery looked almost empty.

'Hi . . . Premji, how are you?'

'Fine . . . What about you?'

'I am alright . . . Come, let's meet Mom . . . She will give you some Coffee,' he told pleasantly.

'Not now'

Slowly, I walked toward his huge library. Pretty rich parents he has . . . that's why he could spend a minimum of five or six thousands every month to purchase new titles. So possessive he was, on his personal belongings as he never allowed anyone to lend a book from that library.

'Raw Youth,' a novel by Feodor Dostoevsky, was lying on the table. I had to complete that book just by sitting there years back!

'To Premji . . . With Love . . . Saji,' it was written so artistically on the front page. I couldn't believe my eyes!

'Premji . . . It's for you!'

'Saju . . . when did you become so generous?'

'Just yesterday!' He started laughing. 'I will present one of my paintings also to you . . . My masterpiece . . . What do you say?'

'Sounds great'

'That's Saju . . . Saju the painter!'

'Saju . . . let me ask you a simple question,' I stopped in the middle . . .

'Go forward'

'So . . . When are you going to do that?'

'What?'

'Suicide!'

♥

Saju and me . . . We are friends since childhood . . . He joined Fine Arts College to fulfill his dream and I had to end up in an Engineering college though my mind was busy with unwritten characters.

During my first semester vacations, I went to his college. Young boys and girls were busy sketching nature using charcoal.

'Premji . . . meet my friend . . . Niru,' Saju introduced a beautiful girl. 'Nirupama'

'Hi,'

'Hi Premji . . . I know everything about you,' Nirupama said.

'What is your specialization?'

'I prefer applied arts,' Niru replied.

'And you . . . Saju?'

'Why doubt? Painting . . . painting . . . painting!'

I could see his excitement in her eyes!

Yes! Her eyes were his biggest canvass! They were madly in love!

♥

Four years disappeared like four months . . . Niru was selected by O&V, one of the leading advertising companies of the world, and was appointed in their Bangalore office. She emptied almost half of her salary just for recharging her 3G mobile phone to call Saju. In the meantime, Saju was completely engaged with new paintings . . . He never wanted to leave his parents as he was completely aware of his caliber! Someday, I will also become a known painter!

Gradually the number of calls and e-mails dropped drastically.

'Colors don't have the same vibrancy as of earlier,' someone started telling him. A causeless uneasiness started tormenting him.

♥

They were sitting inside a star hotel in Bangalore. She was enjoying different layers of Cassata ice-cream . . . First layer was over . . . First layer of life!

'Saju . . . I have been selected for O&V's overseas assignments . . . I have to be there in California by Thursday . . . ,' Nirupama said calmly.

'nhum,'

'And I am not sure when will I be back,'

'nhum'

'Will you come with me?'

'No . . . Why can't we stay in Trivandrum itself?'

'That's impossible . . . My career will then be in gutters!'

'Then?'

'Then what? No more emotional commitments, Saju! Bye forever!' Nirupama told boldly.

♥

Saju started crying like a child, hugging me tightly. The iron fist of depression started strangling him again and again . . .

'How did you know that?' he asked through unending sobs.

'Because, I am your friend . . . Your eyes can never lie with me'

'Premji . . . I am so fed up . . . so drained . . . Take me somewhere,' he requested me.

'Loss of love' is the short-cut to madness . . . , his sleepless eyes silently told me.

♥

Sushama was standing in the midst of some aged women, like a Lily among thorns, near that palliative care center when we entered into the campus of Regional Cancer Center.

'Hi Sushama,'

'Hi . . . Premji . . . How are you?'

'Fine . . . Meet Mr. Saju . . . You know . . . he is a wonderful painter'

'Is it?'

'Yes.'

'Thanks God! Mr. Saju . . . will you be able to help me? See . . . one of our patients . . . a very bright girl child . . . She likes to paint, a lot . . . but, I was not in a position to . . . ,' Sushama asked him openly.

'Surely,' he replied immediately.

'That can help her to recover fast,' she said. 'Medicine is for the body . . . But, faith is the best medicine for mind, which only cures every ailment!'

'Faith!'

♥

His painting camp became an instant hit among young patients. Their laughter could easily bring back the colors of his life.

'If you don't like to live for yourself, Then, why can't you try to live for others?'

His mother showed me a piece of paper, which she got from his room.

'He has become a poet now!' we laughed.

♥

Two weeks later . . .

Saju and Sushama were coming down, all alone, through the lift.

'Shall I marry you?' he asked her.

She remained silent for a moment.

'What do you know about me?'

'I know only this . . . that you are the woman whom I love!'

'I am an orphan'

'So what?'

'I was a Cancer patient once'

'So what?'

'I can't bear you a child'

'Anything more?'

'Nothing'

'Then . . . Nothing to worry . . . dear . . . We can adopt a child!'

'Saju . . . every problem has a solution . . . the only thing is . . . we have to find them out in the right time,' she smiled. 'You are alright now'

He hugged her tightly like a raw youth! He could see warm rays of a new colour emanating from her lips!

Is that the colour of hope?

December 05, 2011

28

Super Star

Pandarath Mines is the only lime stone mine in Kerala, situated 3000 feet above sea level and that too inside a dense forest where wild elephants are your best pals! What a crazy place it is! You can touch the clouds with your hands . . . But, in March, you will be thrown into the core of Sun! And during winter, you will be buried in mist immediately after noon!

One day, I was standing in front of the canteen. Lot of gas cylinders were stocked there and the canteen boy came there to pick up one. Careless boy . . . One of the cylinders fell down with a thud.

Zzzzzzzz . . . A four feet long snake lifted his hood in anger . . . We killed it in no time. It was a King Cobra!

'Its mate might be somewhere nearby . . . sure it might take revenge,' one of the tribal men told.

'Let her take revenge,' I lit a cigarette in hiding. I was a graduate apprentice there and was supposed to be decent among senior engineers. Suddenly, Pappettan stopped his heavy duty dumper near to us. He jumped down in a quick move and tried to snatch the Wills cigarette from my mouth. Sad, he won in that attempt. 'Pappettaa, let me have two puffs'

'Sorry Boy . . . Don't spoil your lungs,' he moved away laughing. I couldn't say anything as he was my Guru in driving huge dumpers carrying 35 tons of load. What a gutsy man he is!

♥

'Sir, you will leave us soon,' office peon handed over a call letter from TVS, a large company dealing sales and service of vehicles. I had to attend an interview for the post of Sale engineer at Chennai. Syam was watching the preview of a Tamil movie at Vahini studio, when I rang him over mobile phone. He called back in the interval.

'Premji, how are you man?

'Fine . . . How is life in Kodampakkam*?'

'Still working as an assistant director . . . Mostly in the next movie, I will become an associate director. So, why did you call me?'

'Tomorrow morning . . . I will be there in Chennai . . . You know my father is going to take a movie.'

'Is it true?'

'Yahhhhhh'

'Then I will direct it.'

'Done,' I smiled.

♥

Chennai . . . There I met him for the first time . . . Ratheesh, the room-mate of Syam. A dark Tamil guy . . . but, he had some grace on his face . . . He was working in housekeeping section of a large star hotel. Enough money he had to spend and Syam used to meet his daily expenses through him . . . Who will pay for an assistant Director?

'Syam . . . did you promise him role in a movie?'I asked.

'Don't talk aloud about him . . . He can understand Malayalam'

'You cunning guy . . . You will never get him a role until you are financially safe' . . . We laughed.

I was appointed in Chennai, even though there was a vacancy in Kochi. As our senior manager wanted to groom me as a great sales man, even I too had to end up in their room in Triplicane. Marina beach was a single stone throw away and we used watch beautiful girls during free time in the evenings.

'Premji, this bastard will never get me a chance in movies?'Ratheesh told me one day.

'Sure, he will get you,' I told to avoid a fight between them.

'He was just using me to meet his expenses based on his vain promise'

'So?'

Syam came back with ground nut packets.

'Is some serious discussion going on?'he enquired.

'Yes . . . I will not spend even a single paisa for you from now own . . . Premji, it's your turn to support him,'Ratheesh told in anger.

'Someone should support me,' Syam walked away coolly . . .

'Bastard . . . Every assistant director in Chennai is a parasite . . . Till today; he didn't pay the room rent even for a single month'

'Leave it Rathi'

'OK . . . Rathi . . . What a lousy screen-name . . . he suggested for me . . . it resembles that of a woman.'

'Rathi . . . Your screen name is of very poor numerology . . . that's why you are not getting chances in movies,' I tried to cool his anger . . .

'Premji, please correct the spelling of my name'

'Add one more 'T' in your name'.

From that day he started calling himself as 'Ratthi' . . . Superstar Ratthi! I knew, someday he would fire me too . . .

♥

Days went on without any important happenings. In TVS, our Senior Manager was a wonderful man who used to give me tough tasks . . . Real tough task for a beginner!

'Premji, now listen . . . See, this is a mobile tower crane,' he showed me a brochure; 'we have been trying from past three years to push one. You have to get an order within a month'

'Sir, I will try my level best'

'That's not a positive answer. If you can achieve that, sure I will recommend you for a raise'

'I will Sir . . . Thank you Sir . . . Will you please give me its project report Sir?'

'Yes, of course,' he handed over that from his table drawer. 'Now listen, Premji . . . to achieve any goal in life, add some element of 'Imagination' in that! Creative imagination will lead you to wonderful ideas . . . ideas are the seedlings of success . . . best of luck . . . Boy'

'Thank you . . . Sir'

Lucky enough I was . . . The chief executive of a construction company placed an order and as promised, I got a raise. That Rs. 500 vanished along with urine . . . Idiots drank beer like Camels, which were back after a month long desert journey.

♥

Ratthi and Syam left the room early in the next morning.

'Premji, why didn't you go office?'Syam asked when he returned in the evening.

'How do you know that?'

'I went to your office . . . just to borrow some money . . . I have to find out a new Director as my Guru and mentor . . . Come get me a cup of coffee,'he told as he didn't eat or drink anything that day.

My God! Please give a raise of rupees 3000 more! Ratthi didn't come even after 11.30 PM.

'Syam, where is your superstar?'

'God knows!'

Ratthi was back on the next day morning with a huge swelling on his face.

'Ratthi, what happened?'I asked.

'I have to find a new job,' he told in a sad tone.

God! Please give me a raise of another 3000/—. I was the only earning member in the room. I rang up the star hotel and enquired the details of Ratthie's dismissal. The receptionist told me that funny but sad story. Ratthi gave a huge treat to one of the upcoming movie directors in Tamil. Both of them participated in a stunt scene inside their bar, when drunk heavily. The End! Title cards came up!

They didn't have any control over hotel food and my salary vanished like ether in air! At last, Ratthi started cooking inside the room. Minimum expense! Maximum, thin, porridge!

'Idiots, I cannot support you all life. You both have to find some job at the earliest,' I told in deadly anger. But, who cares. 'Ratthi, try to learn spoken English. Then you can get wonderful jobs' . . .

Ratthi listened to me.

'Syam . . . What about you?'

'A film maker is not supposed to do anything other than that,' escorted with a laugh, he declared his stand.

'OK, then don't drink porridge . . . it is also something other than film making . . . Bastards! You better kill me!

And from on that night, Ratthi started learning Spoken English. He used to read aloud both English as well as it's translation in Tamil till late night . . . He spoiled my nights for almost a month . . . He had to sell every precious property to keep his health in good condition . . . to maintain the super stardom!

♥

And one day, we were walking through Mount Road in Chennai. Ratthi spotted a foreigner and his girlfriend on the other side of the road.

'Come . . . Let's cross the road,' he pulled my hand . . . The traffic was so heavy . . . It was suicidal . . .

'You want us get killed?'

'No . . . I want to talk to them in English,' Ratthi said innocently. 'Talking with a foreigner can improve my English! I want to test my fluency'

'You better watch the movie 'Gone with the wind,' I told.

We closed our eyes and crossed the road . . .

'Bastards . . . are you going to die?' the Bus drivers shouted while ramming the breaks.

At last we reached near the White couple.

'Good Evening Sir . . . Good Evening Madame,'we greeted them warmly. But, Ratthi was silent.

'Good evening,'they told in return.

'Sir I am Premji . . . Syam and he is Ratthi . . . Where are you from . . . Sir?'I asked.

'I am Richard and she is Janet . . . And we are from Holland . . . And we are on the way to Marina beach.'

'O . . . That's great Sir,'Syam told.

'Sir, our friend Ratthi is learning Spoken English now . . . He likes to talk with you.'

'O . . . No problem'

Ratthy cleared his throat and looked at me for some additional confidence. I just nodded my head indirectly telling to go on . . .

'Hello Sir,'Ratthi greeted him.

'Hello,' Richard shook hands with Ratthi, Janet was watching them talk with great curiosity.

'How are you Mr. Richard?'Ratthi asked.

'I am fine,' Richard replied at once. 'So, how are you?'

'Now-a-days, it is very . . . very . . . bad . . . So, pleeeeeeese give me 50 Rupees . . . ,' Ratthi replied in a sad tone.

♥

'Syam . . . where are they?' I asked . . .

'There they are,' he showed an unusual scene . . . The White couple was trying to avoid vehicles while frantically crossing the Mount Road. They both got into an Auto-rickshaw

'Take us to the nearest Airport,' Richard shouted aloud . . .

We were laughing like anything . . .

'Tourists! What kind of tourists? Indians also go abroad as tourists . . . But, only very rich people! It seems, they both visited India using unemployment wages! With $15, they can enjoy a whole day here and with that can't even have breakfast in Europe. Our nation has no use from such tourists!,' Ratthi told burning with anger . . .

'Ratthi, you told the truth man . . . Superstar you are!'

July 07, 2011

29

The Last Smile

'Albert's Birthday,' Kunjamma Joseph told herself while deleting the remainder from her basic model mobile phone. She felt a twinge of pain in her heart when she spelled out his name. How can a woman forget her one and only son, though he was not with her for the past three years.

'They will be here within twenty minutes. Kunjumon called me just now. Is lunch ready?' seventy year old Joseph chettan asked his wife.

'Everything is ready except 'Karimeen pollichathu' (steamed Pearlspot fish),' she replied coldly.

An old Maruti 800 car stopped in front of his old house, adjacent to a beautiful lake.

'Hi Uncle . . . here is your gift,' the new relative handed over a bottle of VAT69 to him

'Thank you . . . son . . . Come in young lady,' Mr. Joseph welcomed the pretty couple in.

'Please change your clothes and freshen up yourself,' the old woman told them while serving chilled tender coconut water. 'You can use that room . . . We can talk peacefully during lunch'. She couldn't move away her eyes from the expensive Gold ornaments on the young woman's neck and ears.

Tender coconut water ran down her stomach like a cold stream of relief and she moved into the guest-room. Though he followed her closely, he had to stand outside as she had latched the door from inside.

'Shy girl,' the old woman smiled at him.

The guest room was spacious enough and the bathroom fittings were a bit expensive. Earlier, it was used by Albert and his beautiful wife. Though water from shower pierced her naked body like thin needles, she carefully avoided the water spray fall on her hair.

♥

Back in guest-room, she felt so sleepy after lunch as the aged couple treated them like guests of honour. He went into the bathroom just to wash his mouth again and again using mouth freshener. A foul smelling mouth is the greatest foe of every youngster!

He sat near her on the bed and started caressing her long fingers looking into her beautiful eyes and she became an embodiment of shyness! He was waiting for this moment . . . this much privacy from many days! She closed her eyes tightly when he kissed every inch of her naked body . . .

'So beautiful you are! Safe period now?' he asked in her ears.

'Yes,' she replied without opening her eyes. Like wandering thoughts, her shampooed hair, for the first time in her life, danced in air from the fast moving fan blades.

A quick movement . . . Her beautiful face became tight with exorbitant pain. She tried to push him away in quick reflex. But, lust makes a man an absolute beast!

Within no time, hot blood started painting the portrait of lust on the pale blue bed-sheet . . . Unfortunately, it kept on enlarging . . .

♥

'Nothing to worry . . . bleeding has stopped,' well known Gynaecologist Dr. Sathi told Kunjamma Joseph, who stood out in tension, in that evening.

'Thank you Madam'

'You son is lucky . . . tell him not to be so rough again to that virgin,' Dr. Sathi teased her while walking away.

♥

Mr. Kunjumon, fifty year old fishing boat captain, sat on the deck watching the sea-birds moving up from the water level with fishes in between their beaks in the morning. Lucky birds, he thought . . . His boat, with a 400HP Chinese diesel engine, was lying idle as forty five day long trawling ban was going on . . . Huge boats can easily hamper the breeding season of fishes, he knew that much better than anyone. Slowly he sank into deep slumber. A mobile phone call interrupted his peaceful sleep and he went in search of the caller.

Being someone regularly wrestling with the sea, he believed in truth, honesty and personal dignity . . . 'Otherwise Mother Sea would abandon me in the most needed hour . . . ,' his inner-conscience kept on warning him every moment.

♥

She was busy removing her gold ornaments when he reached near the car. She tried to smile, but the muscles on her face didn't respond to her mind. While getting out, she handed over the gold ornaments to Kunjumon and sat on the cement bench inside the bus shelter. He was shocked to know that she couldn't walk properly.

'Bastard . . . What the 'fuck' have you done to her?' Kunjumon caught hold of the T-shirt of the young man. 'Get out I say'

'Please calm down Kunjumon Chettaa,' he started pleading . . . 'Please don't ruin me . . . please listen to me,' he was literally afraid of his huge muscles of the boat captain.

'She is not a bitch or anything . . . as you think . . . understand you rotten bastard . . . Poor girl had to sleep with you only to find some money for her Mom's operation . . . to relieve her from chronic pelvic pain . . . She has nothing to sell except this body . . . you pervert raped her brutally,' Kunjumon couldn't hide his anger.

'I will pay . . . how much ever you ask,' he told out of fear.

'What 'I will pay?' . . . What do you think of her? Do you think that she will be doing this for ever? She won't be doing it any more . . . Understand,' Kunjumon couldn't control his anger. 'I just helped her to get a reliable client . . . But . . . you,'

'Forgive him Kunjumon Chettaa,' she cried out from the bus shelter.

Thirty five thousand rupee notes were handed over to Kunjumon, ten thousand rupees in excess from the decided deal.

'Shall I go?' he asked Kunjumon.

'O.K,'

'May I know her name and mobile number?'

'Sorry . . . neither you nor she has a name,' Kunjumon told out of anger. 'Now get lost,'

The young man tried to smile at her while speeding away . . . but, the poor girl was in some other world.

'Joseph Chettaa . . . shall I deposit your share in your bank account?' Kunjumon asked politely though mobile phone.

'I will tell you what to do . . . let me ask her,' he replied from the other end

♥

Kunjamma Joseph closed the marriage album of Albert, her one and only son who works as a Hydraulics engineer in Ahmedabad, a metropolitan city. The dowry he got was not sufficient enough to buy a good flat there and he was forced to request his dad to sell out his own house to serve his purpose, by his newly-wed wife.

'That will be the dead end of my life!' Joseph, the old man, knew his daughter-in-law better than anyone!

'Why don't you ask her parents to do the same? She is also their one and only kid,' he made a simple suggestion to his son.

Her father accepted it with a crooked condition 'Albert . . . forget your parents forever!'

Since then, he stopped supporting his aged parents financially and mentally. Broker Kunjumon emerged as a Saviour as he used to send three or four important customers to the old-man's house every month. It was a mutually beneficial contract as his customers were relieved from the fear of frequent Police raids and the insults connected with. A client can really enjoy sex when his mind is free from all sort of tensions; Kunjumon knew that from the very start of his part-time business! Again, none from that village suspected the old couple as they lead a very devout life. Neighbours thought that the visitors might be their relatives! The old couple didn't have any tension as Kunjumon was a man with principles! To keep the secrecy of his business, Kunjumon avoided even partying with friends!

♥

'Kunjumon, please give my share also to her,' Mrs. Kunjamma Joseph told him over mobile phone. 'I wish . . . she could have been my daughter!'

'I too!' Kunjumon replied painfully.

The young girl left with thirty thousand rupees inside her hand bag. Kunjumon felt a blend of immense happiness and sadness simultaneously. Did I help someone? or . . .

'Forgive me holy mother.'

♥

Soumya, the young girl thanked Sabeena, an abandoned wife, in mind as she only introduced Kunjumon the gentleman to her while returning back by an Auto rickshaw.

♥

'Premji . . . today afternoon, we are going for a long drive,' my bosom friend Jaison announced loudly, while having lunch at home.

'That's O.K . . . But, no 'drinks' while driving,' my wife interrupted in the middle. 'When you people go out, you don't even think of the women and children at home.'

'This is the real problem . . . soon you are going to understand that . . . ,' I laughed. 'Jaison . . . a man is going to get married just to answer three questions, almost every day!'

'Sounds interesting,' Jaison said.

'Where are you going? Why do you go? When will you be back? Is that clear?' my elder son told loudly as if reciting something from his memory!

'Great training . . . my friend,' Jaison laughed aloud.

'O.K . . . You drive,' he told me while tossing the keys to me.

How come a auto-freak like him handing over the keys to me, that too a novice-driver like me? I was wondering all the way desperately trying to tame that metal beast made by Toyota Corporation. Soon he started snoring, leaning on to the door glass.

'Idiot,'

It was around nine'o clock in the evening and bottle of Smirnoff Vodka was almost over. I felt very sleepy sitting in the veranda of that beach resort. The mild wind from the sea started rocking me very slowly.

'Idiot . . . open your eyes,' Jaison sprinkled some ice-water on my face. 'I have taken you all the way just to discuss something really important'

'Impotent?'

'If you drink Vodka like this, naturally that's going to be your fate!'

♥

Dubai . . . Jaison was celebrating his 34th birthday with his best pals in an expensive hotel in Dubai. Friends were busy emptying expensive bottles as they were the participants in some boozing competition and he was thinking about the curves and straights of his life so far in Dubai. Fifteen years . . . he worked day and night to build up his dream business empire. Jaison was a role model of every

Indian boy new to Dubai since he rose up from humble beginnings! And he remained humble as ever . . .

'Jaison, when are you going to get married?' someone brought him back to the present moment.

'Not yet decided,'

'Most men fail to take the most important decision of his life,' Samuel a fifty year old divorcee opined.

'What's that?' Jaison asked curiously.

'Whom to marry!'

Everyone applauded his argument . . .

'Jaison . . . do you have that experience?' Manoj Nair asked.

'What experience?'

'Russian girls!'

'No,'

They all laughed at him mercilessly!

'I will introduce Kunjumon . . . He will take care of the rest . . . cent percent . . . you can believe him . . . ,' Samuel laughed loudly.

♥

It was a sunny morning, a week after his first encounter with Saumya. Jaison stood under the shower for more than ten minutes in his native home. He tried to recollect every beautiful female face whom were the active part of his solo-sport earlier! But, every face resembled that of Saumya.

Is there still the smell of her blood? He washed his hands again and again.

Another week passed . . . He stood again in the bathroom, that too after having that magical 'blue tablet' . . . Poor man couldn't locate an imaginary mate for his solo-sport! He failed bitterly!

♥

'Shall we fix it or not?' You should give an answer within three days . . . ,' his Mom gave him an ultimatum.

'I will tell you later,' he replied without any interest.

'What can I do with a limp . . . shit,' he cursed himself.

I woke up early in the morning as my I became the apt synonym for thirst! Not even one litre mineral water could satisfy my body! Every joints of my body was aching to the core. Again, desperately I tried to continue my sleep.

'Premji . . . are you awake?' Jaison asked.

'Didn't you sleep properly in the night?'

'No . . . I can't sleep properly now-a-days,' he said painfully. 'Every moment, I feel more and more lethargic . . . please tell me a way-out?'

'What way out?' I kept on changing the cable TV channels and hopefully, he looked on my face. At last, I could select a channel where my favourite movie was about to start.

'Though you live in Dubai, you are not a globalized businessman . . . You still carry the overburden of values! That's your problem!'

'I know . . . I know,'

'Now watch this . . . ,' I went back to sleep . . .

The title card of the movie appeared on the TV screen.

♥

'Plants are million times better than human beings!' Joseph chettan told himself while watering the vegetable plants in the evening. He closed the water tap when a car stopped in front of his home.

'Hello Joseph Uncle,' Jaison greeted

'I have stopped that stupid business . . . please don't trouble me gentleman,' old man told stubbornly, watching Saumya—the young woman—wearing enough gold ornaments, getting out of the car.

'Bye . . . Uncle . . . Have a nice day,' Jaison told calmly and walked towards the car. The old man picked up the water hose again.

'Joseph Uncle,' Soumya greeted him loudly.

'Sorry,' he told while opening the tap.

'What about a honeymoon couple?' Saumya walked in boldly . . .

A gentle smile appeared on the old man's face after three years!

February 17, 2012

30

School-Rags

Sabu and his beloved wife stood near the altar of that ancient church, consecrated in the name of St. George. None of his relatives were present during the baptizing ceremony of Annie, his one and only daughter, except me.

'Sabu, bring her up like a devout Christian . . . ,' he tried to recollect the only request put forth by his mother in law, that too in her death bed. 'Let her grow up as a God fearing girl . . . ,' poor woman closed her eyes.

He was forced to do so since he is a Hindu and Suja Xaviour, his belove wife, is a Christian. She is working as a highly paid nurse in one of the high profile Hospitals in Florida. He didn't have a permanent job and poor man was donning days just like a parasite.

'Stupid love affair!' he cursed his financial insecurity . . .

Poor man was completely aware of the secret dream of his wife, unfortunately it coined with her mother! It took nearly five years for a simple, but, crucial decision! Unfortunately, they were forced to return in connection with last days of his mother-in-law, that too after seven years of marriage.

'Tell him not to worry . . . even, I too am an outcast like him!' St. George* told me silently.

♥

Father Zacharias started reciting some stanzas from Holy Bible. With atmost love and care, he sprinkled holy water on the five year old Annie's forehead.

'Are you pouring cold water on my head? You idiot!' the little girl started shouting aloud and everyone was shocked of her unexpected move, resulting in pin-drop silence.

'Ha . . . ha . . . ha . . . , at last I could meet an intelligent kid,' a retired Vicar proclaimed happily. 'Let her be in our school, till she is leaving for US.'

♥

'Premji, you must meet me today,' Principal of the school, where both of my sons are studying, demanded over phone.

'Sir, I will make myself free so that I can meet you on Saturday . . . You know, my casual leaves are already over,'

'No excuses Mister . . . You must be here in my office on or before 3PM . . . today . . . ,' he slammed the phone.

'Shit'

♥

Five year old Annie sat on the front bench. Amar, my younger son, a notoriously mischievous lad, sat next to her.

'Hello,' he greeted her with great enthusiasm and to his distress; she didn't care him at all.

'After all, she is from America,' Father Zachariah felt a pinch of happiness deep within and a crude smile appeared on his face.

'Fatherrrr . . . I will teach you a lesson,' Amar was deeply hurt.

He sat closer to the little girl, and kissed her beautiful left arm, in a quick move!

'Chee!' a voice of protest escaped from her angry mouth and she wiped her left hand on her long skirt, again and again; later with a hand kerchief . . .

'There is no point in wiping your hand . . . That kiss will remain etched on your heart, forever!,' Amar told her like a 'loving' villain in a romantic movie.

'You deserved it, young lady,' Father Zachariah couldn't control his laughter.

November 14, 2012

31

Antiques

'Premji . . . She is the latest arrival to my fleet,' seventy year old Mr. Raman Menon showed me a vintage Chevrolet Buick Car, that too in showroom condition, with humble pride!

'Black Vintage beauty! Is she 'the one' among those two Buicks remaining in Kerala?'

'Absolutely . . . Her first owner was a Prince from Cochin dynasty . . . Eight cylinder metallic beast . . . But, her lust for gas is horrible . . . just two kmpl . . . but . . . You have to ride her! What a performance!'

Suddenly his mobile started vibrating.

'A call from Azeez!'

I could immediately spot a lovely glow emanating from his face during the conversation.

'Sir . . . anything new?'

'Yes . . . Premji, are you free today?'

'Yes Sir'

'Then . . . Let's go to Chalai Bazar,' Mr. Menon almost shouted with exhilaration.

♥

Every nook and corner of his house was flooded with antiques! Only the rich are destined to do crazy things like this! They can only dictate their material life!

Mr. Menon carefully selected a key from his special room in that huge garage where the log books, shop manuals, registration certificates and all other documents related to his collection were kept. I stood near the door counting the antique cars.

'Twenty one . . . including this,' Mr. Menon told while pointing towards a Scoda tricycle. 'I got it from Delhi . . . in India, it's with me only!'

Is this man crazy?

♥

Mr. Raman Menon drove an open top Mahindra Perol Jeep very fast.

'Premji . . . do you know . . . how many great leaders . . . including Presidents and Prime Ministers . . . accepted guard of honour by standing on this jeep! I bought her for just fifteen thousand rupees ($300)'

'Great'

The vehicle entered into Chalai Bazaar, one of the oldest bazaars in Kerala where everything is available. Chalai Bazaar . . . It has been functioning for centuries!

'Vehicle parking is so difficult here,' Mr. Menon told while fitting the jeep into a tight place near that antique shop.

Mr. Azeez was standing in front of his shop as if he was awaiting us.

'Welcome Sir'

'Azeez . . . show them to me . . . ,' Mr. Menon ordered hastily.

♥

'So . . . Jaa . . . So . . . Jaa . . . Rajkumari . . . So . . . Jaa,' (Sleep off . . . Princess . . . Sleep off), the magical voice of K. L. Sehgal started flooding inside that small room, from a very old gramophone record.

'Sir . . . this is . . . one among the first set of records by KL Sehgal . . . nearly seventy years old! I got it from a musician's family in Nagarcoil . . . ,' Azeez told proudly as if he had done some sacrifice for Mr. Menon!

'Azeez . . . you know me much better than anyone,' Menon congratulated him while settling the deal. 'Premji . . . let's go to Salim's 'aacri' shop . . . I have to search for some old clutch plates'

♥

Mr. Menon started his jeep.

'Sir . . . Shall I ask you something?'

'Surely . . . Premji'

'What will happen to your antiques collection . . . after your life?'

♥

Three days back . . .

Mr. Menon was supervising that Bangali servant boy, doing water service on his 1935 model Dodge Car, in the morning. Mrs. Menon was busy pruning imported Rose plants.

'Good Morning Sir . . . Good Morning Madam,' Mr. Syamalan, a Pranic Healing expert, greeted him while parking his scooter in front of his house.

'Good Morning,' he greeted back without much interest.

'Welcome Mr. Syamalan,' Mrs. Menon took him inside.

'Have you noticed his face?' Mrs. Menon asked her husband when Mr. Syamalan had left, immediately after her treatment.

'What is there to see on his face?'

'The glow . . . the splendor . . . the aura . . . You know . . . every day, he cleanses negative energy from his body . . . his cheeks are so rosy because of that! That's the effect of Pranic Healing!'

'My foot! That's because he drinks a lot!'

'You are jealous!'

'Hell! That too in this age! You better talk something else'

'I feel quite relaxed today . . . holistic treatment can do wonders . . . my knee pain is getting reduced!'

'Reduce your body weight before reaching into conclusions,'

'Everything is because of your crazy passions . . . ,' Mrs. Menon told bit arrogantly.

'What?'

'Those lousy antiques . . . they bear a lot of negative energy! And that negative energy, got transferred in to my body! That only causes all sort of health problems to me . . . since I am the weakest person in this house!'

'Bastard,' Mr. Menon took out an antique gun from the wall and reserved a bullet for Dr. Syamalan.

♥

'Premji . . . what did you ask me?'

'Sir . . . What will happen to these antiques after your life?'

'What will happen? They all will reach here!' he told sadly while pointing towards the antique and 'aacri' shops in Chalai Bazaar!

*Pranic Healing is an alternative medicinal practice that claims to use prana or life energy to heal ailments in the body.[1] Ancient cultures practiced similar modes of healing known as shamanic healing, divine healing, healing by mantra, among others. In 1995, Jack Ruso described the method in the magazine Skeptical Inquirer as 'mystical or super-naturalistic'.Pranic Healing can be used to increase the rate of healing in both minor and major ailments. However, it should not be treated as a substitute for conventional medicine. One must consult a physician/specialist to get a proper medical treatment. Pranic healing is complementary to a proper medical treatment.

December 13, 2011

32

English

'A NEW STUDENT HAS joined our class, Mom . . . You know . . . she speaks only English,' my five year old son started shouting, while getting down from school Bus.

'Son, you better have good friendship with her so that you can also speak English fluently,' my wife encouraged him.

'But, how can I speak to her? I know just *'one English'* . . . you only taught me that . . . But, she cannot answer to my 'one English'.'

'What is that?'

'Teacher, may I go to the toilet?'

We laughed a lot . . .

Globalization crowns English as 'World language'. Sad, every local kid has to bury his dreams in the dirty waters of inferiority complex!

July 02, 2011

33

Never Help A Woman

I used to visit my friend's Internet cafe frequently as I have no net connection at home. I had been there for quite some time, day before yesterday as I couldn't check my mails for a week because of Tomato fever . . . what all fevers! God!

Right on the desktop, a MS Office word file was kept open . . . It was the bio-data of a woman named Lakshmi of age 28 . . . She holds a Master's degree in Malayalam . . . Currently doing a course in journalism . . . Selected as best citizen journalist by a local TV channel . . . Winner of several literary awards and beyond all, she was a nearby girl . . . Her photograph revealed her lovely face! I noted down her mobile number and deleted the whole.

Later, in the evening, I told about her in our family . . . My mother-in-law was very much interested as my brother-in-law (37) is still unmarried . . . He too is a screenplay writer . . . She forced me to call her and I did call . . .

'Hello Ms. Lakshmi, I am Premji, calling from so and so place . . . I come forward with a marriage proposal for you.'

'Mr. Premji, from where did you get my phone number?'

'I got it from a bio-data left open in a net cafe'

'How can that be possible? I deleted that immediately after typing it . . . You might have done some fraud.'

'Excuse me miss . . . mind your words.' I slammed my mobile . . .

Everyone at home, were laughing at me . . .

'Idiot, better fall in love with some woman,' I shouted at my brother-in-law.

My mobile started ringing after five minutes . . . This time her uncle was on the other end . . .

'It seems you called my niece?'

'Yes'

'You went through her bio-data?'

'Yes'

'See, she attached that to an e-mail and deleted. If you got it means, you might have downloaded it by hacking into her e-mail id. See, even I too use computers for years . . . What you have done is a crime according to Indian Cyber law'

'No way . . . Your niece doesn't know how to delete a file permanently . . . tell her press shift and delete next time'

'Then why did you call her?

'For a marriage proposal for my brother-in-law.'

'I don't think so . . . Young men like you, never allow young women live peacefully . . . We are not going to leave you anyway. Be careful.'

♥

My mobile got barred on the very next day . . . Citizen Journalist played her trump card! She can write and give anything as complaint . . . Like verbal sexual abuse or anything! Women have several cards . . .

My wife handled the matter with such an ease like plucking a flower bud . . . She called the uncle from a local telephone booth and told him: 'Sir, you are going to spend your life time in jail.'

'Why?'

'The mobile number that got barred is in my name and you talked 7.5 minutes to that number yesterday. Even I have drafted my complaint. Have a happy, jobless life!'

'Madammmmm'

Citizen journalist pulled back her complaint in no time. We laughed a lot after moments of tension.

'Premji, a man can pay and enjoy a beautiful female body . . . But, none can pay and get a beautiful mind . . . True woman is a beautiful mind . . . You tried to help her with good intention . . . See what happened . . . Why educated women are acting like this? God knows . . . Now, promise me.'

'What promise?'

'Never ever try to help a woman!'

'Promise . . . My woman of substance,' I hugged her.

June 09, 2011

34

Existentialism

'Existentialism . . . What a lovely word it is!' Rajeevan told in an excited mood . . .

'That's the key-word which spoiled our local literature,' I told in return.

'You should revoke that sentence,' he shouted in anger.

'No way! You crazy poet . . .'

'O.K . . . Then we will meet him today itself. Let him decide.'

'Who?'

'Kunjappan Nair . . . our old critic . . . for he is the one who introduced existentialism to our people'

'OK . . . That's a good idea,' I told.

♥

We took a local bus to his village. Old man is a great orator! I had solid doubt: will he be accessible? Does he have any programme today?

My doubts were baseless. He was busy reading some book while lying in an easy chair.

'Good afternoon Sir,' my friend told.

'O . . . Rajeevan . . . How are you?'

'Fine Sir . . . This is my friend Premji'

'Is he a writer?'

'No . . . But he has some doubts about existentialism'

'OK . . . I will just freshen up and come back in ten minutes . . . till then you wait here.'

'Sir, shall I show him your library?'

'As you like,' the old man walked away.

It was a palatial building and the old man is still a bachelor. There were no rooms in the first floor of that building . . . only huge rack racks containing priceless books . . . a great collection he has . . . Rajeevan showed me the very old editions of Kafka, Camus and so on . . . I was simply calculating the area of that library . . . 1500 square feet . . . my calculation . . . very correct . . . and the books worth Rs.5 Million!

I was busy wandering through the space between racks . . . I pushed open a small partition . . . God! What all lovely books kept in hiding . . . Sidney Sheldon . . . John Creasey . . . James Hadley Chase . . . Agatha Christie . . . John Gresham . . . what a sexy collection of popular fiction . . . When I turned back, I saw the old man staring at me . . . His eyes were burning with anger . . . as if I had unearthed a great secret . . .

'Sir, existentialism,'I tried to cool the situation . . .

'What existentialism . . . Kafka and Camus . . . They had it in their soul . . . So, both of them perished early. They (he pointed at the popular fiction racks) protect me still alive from the hands of local Kafka's and Camus . . . Popular fiction will not invoke depression . . . Do you understand?'

'Yes . . . Sir . . . Wishing you 1000 full Moons.'

'Thank you . . . I am already 83'

Then Rajeevan joined us.

'Sir, he has some doubts about existentialism . . . Did he clear them?'

'He doesn't have any doubts at all,' the old man declared loudly.

June 27, 2011

35

In The Name Of God

'Stupid life!'

Forty five year old Kunjunni Nair was having hell a lot of problems to face every day and the worst important thing was his ever-declining financial status. He was in such a spiritual turmoil that he couldn't even analyze the root cause of his eternal suffering!

'Why don't you consult some good astrologer?' one of his well-wishers asked one-day.

Kunjunni Nair sat in front of renowned astrologer Brahmasree Parameswara Menon, to uncover his doomed future, like a faithful dog. Menon took out a conch shell from his bag, prayed for some time and made it revolve on the granite floor. It came to a halt after several seconds of continuous revolution.

'Do you have a temple at your home?' Menon asked.

'Temple?' Kunjunni Nair stopped for a second. 'No . . . We don't have.'

'Any Kavu? (a sacred orchard of huge trees covered with climbers)'

'Yes . . . we have one . . . I think of clear-felling the trees to settle my debt,' replied Kunjunni Nair.

'Please don't even think of that,' Parameswara Menon warned him calmly. 'I can see a 'Chempaka' tree there . . . with lot of flowers . . . She is the abode of 'Devi,' the holy mother . . . You know . . . Your family ignored her for long . . . might be unaware of her presence . . . That's the basic reason for all of your sufferings,'

'What shall I do?'

'Please construct a small shrine for her and try to please her in every possible way . . . She will shower blessings upon your family,' Parameswara Menon declared his final solution of the Nair's problem.

'You have to market everything . . . my dear hubbie . . . Otherwise we cannot repay the loans taken for the temple construction,' Sundanda Nair reminded her husband late in the night.

'Surely . . . I have some plans,' he hugged her tightly.

'No . . . no . . . no pujas tonight,' she tried to release his powerful hands

♥

'Koodanadu Devi: The grace of this house' . . . And from the very next week onwards, he started issuing stickers containing the above statement, absolutely free of cost! They appeared on buses, trains and almost every household nearby. Gradually, Her fame kept on growing . . . Koodanadu Devi, the Goddess was so powerful, that devotees started dropping coins and bundles of notes in-order to please her.

The family temple, owned by Kunjunni Nair, transformed into a colossal structure made of steel and concrete. Thirty five feet, gold plated, flag-post protected her from the wrath of heavy lightening.

At last, he was forced to purchase a brand new e-class Mercedes Benz to do justice to his new found economic status.

♥

'What a change!' thirty eight year old Kunjimooza couldn't believe his eyes while getting out of the taxi car. He had been away, working in Saudi Arabia, for the past ten years. Kadeesumma, his aged mother was happy to receive him as she had almost forgotten his face, her one and only son.

She had been staying, all alone, inside that huge house next to the temple. He was not interested to share the details of his past as every bone inside his body was aching due to jet-lag. He got up, only after thirty six hours of long sleep, listening to a Hindu Hymn from the nearby temple.

'Mooza . . . you want some coffee?' asked the old woman, while opening the windows wide open.

'Yes . . . Umma'

'O.K,' Kadeesumma, stood near the window watching the hundreds of lit up wicks in and around the temple as if she was in a prayer.

'Umma . . . What are you doing? It's against Islam,' the super-religious Muslim in Kunjimooza cried out.

'Son . . . Light emanates when you light up a wick, a candle or incense stick . . . Light . . . Worship the inner-light . . . my son . . . that's Him . . . Allah!' she started walking towards the kitchen.

♥

Within just two weeks, Kunjimooza got married to a country girl. Noorjahan, the bride, was a very beautiful woman of twenty. Since she was from very poor backgrounds, her only personal asset was her stunning beauty. Kadeesaumma was very happy as the bride relieved her totally from every household duty. She had immense patience to listen to the stories of Kadeesumma, specially the stories of her earlier hardships.

♥

'Her menstrual cycle repeats as usual,' Kadeesumma started worrying a bit as three months passed without even a slightest change in her daughter-in-law's tummy.

'She will get pregnant soon . . . Nothing to worry Kadeesumma,' Sunanda Nair consoled her . . . 'After-all, she is a very lean girl! I will light a ghee lamp for her,'

'Let Him bless her'

♥

Kunjimooza returned on the very next week as his four months leave was over. Kadeesumma and Noorjahan spent their life watching the stinking episodes of mega-serials in the television and eating heavily.

'If they stop telecasting these filthy serials glorifying extra-marital affairs, sex abuse of women would be reduced by considerable amount,' opined the old woman out of distress.

♥

'Premji . . . I need some professional advice,' said Sunanda Nair, while handing over a steaming cup of coffee to me.

'About what?'

'Anitha, my daughter, is doing the last semester of her engineering degree . . . Will you please give some ideas about her higher studies?'

'Let her do MBA . . . Master of business administration . . . with a specialization in temple management!' I tried to tease her.

'That's a good option,' she started laughing.

♥

Kunjimooza and his Noorjahan sat before Dr. Sathi Raghavan, a noted gynecologist and infertility specialist during, his next leave.

'What's your age?' she asked him calmly.

'I turned forty last month . . . Madam,'

'She is perfectly all-right . . . So, we should check your sperm count and motility.'

♥

Anitha Nair completed her executive MBA with flying colours.

♥

'Coconut price is falling every day,' Kunjunni Nair was bit worried as he was not getting good price for the coconut yield from his ten hectare coconut plantation.

'Anitha . . . do you have any ideas to improve the popularity of our temple?' asked Sunanda Nair.

'Yes Mom . . . We have to attract more women to improve the temple revenue . . .'

And from the very next Tuesday onwards, 'narangavilakku,' a Hindu ritual was started in their temple. Young girls from different places started visiting the temple with ripe lemons for getting good husbands. Mothers with unmarried daughters visited the temple for good son-in-laws. Married woman participated in 'narangavilakku' for a peaceful family life. They all cut open the lemon into two halves, removed the juice and seeds, inverted the lemon half using their thumps, poured 'holy oil' from the temple (extracted from their coconut plantation), lit a wick inside and placed them all around the temple.

'Amme Narayana . . .

Devi Narayana . . .

Lakshmi Narayana . . .

Bhadre Narayana,'

Later, they started chanting the sacred mantra of the holy mother

As Anitha's agents kept on appearing the local television networks in praise of the temple, the temple revenue increased up to four folds! And she purchased a handsome Tusker and renamed him as Koodanadu Balanarayanan. In order to meet the expenses to feed the elephant, she started another ritual named 'Aanayoottu' (feeding the temple elephant for bliss!' Soon she acted in a musical video about the temple, directed by one of the most famous ad-makers from Kerala.

'Idea means money!'

♥

The sperm count as well as the motility was below the average in case of Kunjimooza as he had been working as a heavy equipment operator in Arabia. Usually, the construction sites were deep inside the deserts and his testicles faced extreme weather conditions. Noorjahan was forced to cool them by applying ice-packs around them in the afternoons.

'If you really need a child, you should be with her at least a year,' Kadeesumma told her son as he had plans to go back to the desert.

'One year?' doubted her son.

'Yes,'

'But . . . my job?'

'Job? What job? Being a lawful husband, your primary job is to make her pregnant,' replied the old woman out of uncontrollable temper.

♥

At last, Dr. Sati Raghavan was successful in separating quite a few number of good quality sperms and they were soon fused with ovum collected from the delicate womb of Noorjahan. And within almost two weeks, her blood as well as urine test results started showing hormonal changes. Yes, the girl was pregnant!

'In-shah Allah!' her mother-in-law cried out . . . 'It will be baby

♥

Kunjimmooza left on the very next week for his beloved desert. Kadeesumma took over the control of the household again. Her expertise in cuisine was clearly visible on the young body of Noorjahan as her tummy kept on growing.

'Six more months,' Kadeesumma folded her thin fingers carefully . . . 'In-shah! Allah!'

♥

'One more month for the temple festival,' Anitha told herself . . . 'What shall we introduce new this year?'

'What about a carnival in the temple ground . . . which can attract lot of children?' opined her mother.

'That's OK . . . but, we need something more memorable . . . something like a small 'Pooram*,' opined Anitha.

'We can go forward with a great 'vedikkettu' (firework extravaganza),' opined her father.

'But . . . it should be worth minimum of one million rupees . . . What do you say?' said the young girl out of uncontrollable enthusiasm.

'Be it so!' assured her father.

♥

Firework expert Kunjikkelu Asan accepted a hundred thousand rupees as token advance from the beautiful hands of Anita. His feeble hands were as dark as coal since he had been handling gun powder from his very childhood. He was one among the key members of the firework experts for 'Thrissur Pooram,' the most coveted firework extravaganza of South-India.

'We will try to introduce some new items here,' said Kunjikkelu politely.

'You should,' replied Anitha . . . 'Don't worry about the expenses . . . It should be a memorable event . . . You should create a marvel in the skies'

Koodanadu Pooram, the Temple festival started with flying colours and the people from the nearby and faraway places kept on visiting in large numbers. Caparisoned elephants added glamour and a bit of terror. Hundreds of oil lamps fixed on the temple walls were lit in the evening.

'What a beautiful sight!' Kadeesumma watched every event from her terrace.

'Absolutely,' said Noorjahan.

And around eight'o clock, the cultural programmes started. Children from the nearby music and dance schools started performing their expertise,'arangettam' . . . their first performance . . .

Kadeesumma felt really sad as Muslims were not allowed to enter into the Hindu temples . . . But, she could see everything more clearly than any spectator.

'Umma . . . I am feeling very sleepy,' said Noorjahan in a feeble voice.

'O.K . . . Dear . . . I am going to watch the entire festival . . . from here' said the old woman.

Soon 'Ganamela'—a music program by one of the most famous music groups started. Kadeesumma felt extremely happy as the music band contained so many noted playback singers. Their faces were so familiar to her through the TV. The programme spanned for almost four hours and the crowd was thrown into some sort of musical frenzy.

♥

It was nearing two, early in the morning.

'Vedikkett' (firework extravaganza) by noted firework expert Kunjikkelu Asan and team will start within ten minutes,' Anitha Nair announced through the loudspeakers.

Kadeesumma was patiently waiting for the same event from the very day she heard about it from Sunanda Nair. She walked downstairs swiftly in-order to wake her daughter-in-law up. She was sleeping peacefully, totally unaware of things happening around.

'Let her sleep,'

Fireworks started, immediately after Kadeesumma settled back on the on terrace . . .

♥

The temple was overflowing with thousands of Pooram fans. Anitha was determined to provide the crowd with the amazing display of pyro-techniques as the culminating item of the Koodanadu pooram. 'Amittu, poothiri, lathiri, vaanam etc—the colourful sparklers lit the sky up with magnificent colours . . . Aerial repeaters, aerial shells, display tubes, firecrackers, flying spinners, fountains, ground spinners, mines, novelties, parachutes, rockets, missiles, roman candles, strobes, sparklers and the wheels . . . It was an exciting and nail biting experience.

And the next item was 'Gundu' (a firework that creates maximum sound with a thud!). The huge containers with highly explosive materials, safely secured on the ground, released thermal energy in the form of hot gases produced by the fast combustion of the black powder, created the sound, the echo and the burning smell!

'Yaa . . . Allah!' Kadeesumma closed her ears with her feeble hands.

The firework was over and Kadeesumma started walking downstairs. But, she was shocked to see her daughter-in-law lying in a pool of blood, fainting. She had a miscarriage!

'I am sorry Mrs. Noorjahan,' said Dr. Sathi Raghavan after carefully checking her delicate womb . . . 'We have to remove the debris as early as possible to avoid further complexities'

'I must talk to my son,' said Kadeesumma.

'How did this happen? Did you have any sudden shock or so, dear Noorjahan?' asked the doctor.

'I was terrified by the fireworks' replied Noorjahan

'Specially the 'garbham kalakki*' cracker,' her mother-in-law added though she was burning with guilt.

(*pregnancy-spoiler!)

♥

Firework expert Kunjikkelu Asan and team were brutally attacked by a group of young religious fanatics, which resulted in a communal riot between Muslims and Hindus. There were losses on both the sides. Soon, Koodanadu was under curfew. The elephants got trapped in the temple ground started roaring mercilessly for food and water.

'Who told them to do such a heinous act?' Kadessumma asked herself as she was so saddened by the mishaps . . . And the most hurting thing was the permanent loss of her one and only friend . . . Sunanda Nair . . .

♥

The debris from Noorjahan's womb was carefully removed and soon she was shifted into a pay-ward. She was still sleeping when Kunjimooza arrived. He sat next her and started pressing her pale fingers, in tears.

'I will teach him a lesson . . . I will,' he started prattling like a madcap.

'Have you gone crazy?' asked his mother impatiently . . . 'Those mindless idiots created enough havoc . . . The whole village is cursing me, though I am totally innocent'

'Whatever it is . . . I will construct a mosque next to the temple, in our own land . . . completely on my own expenses . . . Let our people pray there . . . let the Muslims bury their dead-bodies there . . . Nobody is going to ask me, why I am doing this . . . None can stop me,' Kunjimooza was burning with anger.

'You are mad . . . If, you would have lost your child after its birth, what would you do? You can only do the same . . . sit and lament' She remained silent for a minute. 'You could have avoided this . . . but, you didn't'

'Me?'

'Yes . . . Like every pregnant woman, she too wished to stay in her own home with her parents in your absence. There she gets better care . . . You didn't allow her, only to satisfy your vane pride . . . don't you?'

'But, their financial status is very bad!' Kunjimooza cried out.

'You could have supported them . . . But, you didn't,' the old woman looked outside for some time . . . 'If you want to construct a mosque there, go on with it . . . But, let me warn you . . . Allah, the most kind and merciful, will never . . . never . . . visit there . . . He will never visit a place made of hatred and anger,' Kadeesumma closed her eyes as if she was in a prayer . . .

Kunjimooza remained silent for some-time . . .

'Construct a mosque within your mind . . . my boy,' Kadeesumma touched his face with infinite compassion . . . "and keep it lighted always through prayers!"

A divine smile appeared on his face . . .

The grace of Allah!

April 11, 2013

36

Hero In Real Life

'Sir, I was bitten by a rat yesterday night'

'First, it was Chicken pox . . . now, rat bite . . . Premji, you better try to get a transfer from this place,' our Principal told with a smile. 'Anyway, did you consult any Doctor?'

'No Sir . . . Is that necessary?'

'Absolutely . . . See, you are bitten by a rodent'

'Sure Sir . . .'

♥

I have been sharing that rented house, a tiled house with more than fifty years of unwritten history, with my colleague Jagan. Our house owner kept all his personal belongings in two good rooms and the rest of the house was given for rent! The best portions are always reserved! What a cunning world it is!

Yesterday, I was all alone at home and it was raining cats and dogs. Power failure happened as rain and power remain eternal foes in our little town and I started shivering due to the small rain induced cold-wave! What else to do except sleeping early during lonely times? I used to sleep on the dining table, converted to a temporary bed, in dining room as we have only two rooms for use. My friend went home for 'wifing' and I thought of enjoying the luxury of his warm foam bed and better security of his room.

He was sleeping near me enjoying the warmth of my body and unknowingly I put my left hand on his body. He attacked me in panic and I saw him rushing away through the TV cable. I examined the wound in torch-light and still I am in great confusion: whether bitten or scratched?

Rat attack . . . Rat fever . . . A fear-wave passed through my spine . . .

♥

I was sitting alone in my personal room and my colleagues came there to put signatures on the attendance register. Eight people assembled near me and I told the same episode to them. They started laughing while cracking funny comments.

'Sir, let's go,' Pradeep said. 'There is a community health center near-by'

'Government doctors are better and more efficient than private hospital doctors,' Kishore said.

'The products of private medical colleges are absolutely useless,'Suresh supported him.

'Anyway, arrange the classes for students in my absence,' I told them and while leaving with Pradeep.

♥

Pradeep rode his 100 CC bike very fast. He was very fond of that old Yamaha RX 100 two stroke bike.

'Five dozes of Rabies injection will cost around Rs.2500/—I checked that in the internet,' I said.

'A small rat can destroy our family budget,' he laughed. 'Poor government employees!'

♥

Nobody was there near the community health center. It was orphaned as the duty doctor was on long leave.

'Pradeep, let's go to the nearest private hospital'

'Sir, I will take you to a better place'

And at last we were there at the Government district hospital, after a long ride of 14 km. There was a pretty long queue in the Out-patient (OP) counter. You need a minimum of two hours to get an OP ticket.

'Sir, let me try to locate some known faces,' he walked away.

I stood there in the queue, covering my mouth and nose to protect myself from contacting with fever.

'Sir, please get of the queue,' he told over mobile phone and I did the same. An ambulance driver, in uniform, came near me and handed over an OP ticket. Pradeep came near with a naughty smile on his face.

'Pradeep, how did you manage this?'

'Simple . . . I told him that you are a Police Inspector . . . Your body-language is exactly same as that of a Policeman,' he told while pointing towards a Police jeep parked nearby.

'That's interesting'

He managed myself get examined by doctors at the earliest, that too without standing further in any long queues.

'You can take calculated risks in life. But, this risk is beyond every calculation, Mr. Premji,' the young woman Doctor told while prescribing four dozes of Anti-Rabies injections, TT and some anti-biotics.

'Please pay Rs.10/—for stamps,' Nurse, in the injection room, told while writing down my address in the thick anti-rabies register.

'How much should I pay for the injections?'

'They are of free of cost,' she said while writing down the injection dates on the OP ticket. 'Never fail to take injections on the exact dates. If you fail, then they are of no use,' she cautioned me.

My shoulders bore the pain of three injections and I was reduced to three aching wounds.

'Sir, let's get medicines from pharmacy,' Pradeep said.

Two separate queues were there near the pharmacy for men and women

'Pradeep, your tricks will not work here,' I told him while watching the anger on the faces of women standing in the queue.

'Wait Sir'

'Don't worry, let's buy them from outside.'

'Why Sir, you will get best medicine from here . . . You know why . . . Doctors here don't prescribe anything from outside.'

'That's interesting'

'Those doctors who prescribe poor-quality medicines for huge commissions from local venders are the root cause this sick society,' he pointed towards the queue near the fever clinic. 'Government has no control over them'

'Under qualified doctors treating with under quality medicines . . . that's the hell on earth!'

'They are selling Paracetamol, the simple medicine for fever, in more than thousand brand names. They sell mere clay!' he became angry.

'You are right. In every developed nation, there are only some 105 basic medicines. Doctors decide the combinations and chemists supply the medicines. But, our government support only the manufacturers! They don't care what he manufactures! How sad!'

♥

I felt a bit uneasy while standing in the Medical shop counter. He made me sit on one of the cement benches under a huge tree in the hospital compound.

'Pradeep, how do you know about the in and out of this hospital?'

'Sir, I was a regular visitor of this hospital for fifteen years.'

'Fifteen years?'

'Yes'. He told while taking out a faded black and white photograph from his purse. 'My father . . . he is no more now . . . He was a chain smoker Premji . . . Till the age of fifty, he was there in Dubai . . . Malbero was his favorite brand . . . I tried it once and I couldn't stop vomiting for two days,'he laughed.

'Then?'

'Then bronchial problems developed . . . Whatever he had gained in life, had to be sold for his treatment . . . I lost my studies because I have to accompany him to various hospitals as bystander from the very age of seventeen. . . . Sir, All I could gain as education is just one year certificate course of Automobile engineering . . . that too not by attending the classes regularly! The Principal and teachers had some mercy on me'

'You could have tried for higher studies immediately after getting into government service.'

'I couldn't find time. I did every kind of work, Sir . . . to meet the medicinal expenses of my father . . . our household expenses,' he showed his palms which are hard like rock!

'Pradeep, you are a hero in real life'

'What hero, Sir?' he laughed. 'Sir, I know nothing about your family'

'My family . . . My parents are alive . . . retired teachers . . . father looks after his timber business . . . my sister lives happily with her husband and daughters. I have two sons . . . My wife is a college lecturer'

'Is your sister working?'

'Yes'

'Even I too have a sister . . . I had to bear all her expenses for higher studies and her marriage . . . It was my duty . . . Nobody was there to help me . . . She has a Master's degree in Mathematics now . . . But, she won't write any PSC tests to get a government job . . . Idiot . . . She is happy with a low paid job in a nearby private school . . . Sir, why did I die for her day and night? I am really disappointed Premji'

'You only have to make sure of that . . . whether she applies for PSC tests'

'Premji, I had a debt of eight hundred thousand rupees. I have cleared almost everything . . . now only fifty thousand rupees remaining . . . I do carving of wooden doors in free time, now.'

'Pradeep, I am happy to know that you are an artist'

'I have learned everything from my father. You know Premji, I have sacrificed my life for him,' he told while taking out his father's photograph again. 'But, he defeated me.'

Pradeep was silent for a couple of minutes.

'Yes . . . I gave him the best treatment for fifteen years . . . and of course he was looked after very well by our family . . . he was getting more and more comfortable everyday . . . I used to make his pockets full with money even though he was a spendthrift . . . still.'

'Still?'

'Still, he defeated me by hanging himself . . . in a Mango tree . . . that too planted by me . . . when I was away for job . . . If at all he wanted to commit suicide, he could have done that fifteen years earlier . . . Then my life wouldn't have been like this . . . What is the meaning of life, Premji?'

Fumes of tears were revolving around in his red eyes.

'First Rat bite . . . later Rat race,' we laughed.

The cloud of tears landed on my soul like Acid rain.

August 15, 2011

37

Imaginary Force

'Premji Sir, may I come in?' Sandhya, one of the newly appointed guest lecturers of our college, sought for my permission in the morning.

'Please Come in'

How come this pretty young girl is so uneasy in the morning? A thought flashed through my mind.

'Sir, Rajesh is not at all allowing me to engage classes . . . He is creating a lot of problems, just by asking very silly questions . . . The whole class is getting distracted . . . Please warn him . . . Sir . . . ,' she poured out a gush of her own afflictions!

'Don't worry Sandhya . . . You just relax a bit. Is that O.K?'

'Thank you . . . Sir'

'No need to continue today's classes . . .'

♥

Rajesh stood before me, quite coolly, in the H.O.D room. He is a very intelligent student and wonderful football player.

'Rajesh, please bolt the door . . . I don't want any sort of interruptions while talking with you'

'O.K. Sir'

Rajesh switched off his mobile phone before throwing himself into a seat before me.

'Rajesh, are you comfortable now?'

'Yes . . . Sir'

'O.K . . . Let's come to the point . . . Why do you create problems in lady teacher's classes?'

'Sir . . . I didn't create any problem . . . I just asked some doubts . . . that's all?'

'Is that all?'

'Yes . . . Sir,'

'That's not the reason . . . Do you like her class?'

'Yes . . . Sir'

'Do you like her?'

'Yes Sir'

'Do you love her?'

'No . . . Sir'

'Why?'

'Sir . . . I hate women'

'Do you hate your mother and sister?'

'No'

'O.K. That means you hate some women . . . Who are they?'

'I hate girls . . . especially my classmates . . . I had some soft corner towards Soumya . . . When I told her 'I love you' . . . Sir . . . do you know what was her first response? 'What is your caste?' she asked me openly! Unfortunately my answer was not matching with her caste and I was rejected! Isn't that painful?'

'Surely'

'When I told 'I love you?' to Laila . . . Sir, do you know what did she reply? 'You are not a Muslim,' . . . Sir, isn't that ridiculous?'

'Surely'

'When I told the same to Nancy, she also repeated the same . . . Though love doesn't have any religion, Sir . . . every girl has a reason to reject me! I am really fed up,' Were there liquid stars in his eyes?

'That's true . . . my boy . . . but, one thing you must realize . . . love doesn't happen forcefully . . . it happens spontaneously . . . just like a Rose blooming . . . so natural it is . . . Tell me, how old are you?'

'Sir . . . I am nineteen,'

'I got married at the age of thirty one . . . Why? I just waited for the right woman . . . Patience pays everywhere, young man . . . Try to learn well . . . Get a wonderful job . . . Then, only you can feel the difference . . .'

'You are right . . . Sir . . . Every girl . . . every woman needs security in life! I won't create any more problems in future . . . I promise,'

'That's fine . . . I believe you'

'Thanks Sir'

♥

Dr. Anil, a known psychiatrist and a childhood friend of mine, took us inside his hospital, three weeks later . . . Someone was playing chess with computer, so immersed in the game that he didn't even feel our presence.

'Rajesh,' I touched his back.

'Hello Sir . . . Hello Madam,' he got up immediately.

'How are you?' Sandhya asked.

'I am fine . . . Madam' . . . She was about to cry . . . 'Please don't cry Madam . . . Premji Sir explained everything that day itself . . . But, my mind was not ready to accept . . .

at that time . . . Now, I am alright and I will be back soon . . . Madam,' he was so confident.

'Promise?'

'Yes Madam,'

'Rajesh . . . now, tell me . . . what is love?' Sandhya wiped her eyes.

'Love is an imaginary force which gives acceleration to life!'

December 04, 2011

38

Army Joke

It was a very cold morning in December, and I was traveling by train from Bangalore to Amritsar, the state capital of Punjab. Babri Mazjid—the mosque which remained the core of communal dispute for several decades—was demolished on the previous week by politically motivated Hindu fanatics. The nation was under red alert and as a result, the security inside the trains was tightened.

'Not even a single religion on Earth, can ever offer peace to mankind!' an aged beggar, stood upon the empty platform, cursed himself as he didn't get anything to eat for the past forty eight hours.

Two Punjabi soldiers, going on vacation, were my co-passengers. I was really pestered by their loud discussions followed by rocking laughter.

'Leave us alone,' their rugged muscles, told me silently.

'Premji, better be silent not to get battered!' my conscience warned.

♥

The train covered two or three stations, and a high ranking local Policeman entered into our cabin. Soon, he started talking with the Punjabi soldiers in Hindi. People from Bangalore are so fluent in several languages except Kannada, the official language of Karnataka state! Strange!

After a steaming discussion about the combat status of armed forces, the Policeman started asking very personal questions. The undertone of his questions was mere contempt, I could clearly sense!

'Sardarjis (Punjabis) are the characters in silly jokes, notorious for their foolish acts. He is taking advantage of that,' I told myself. 'And without them, none will eat Wheat in India.'

'O.K. Sardar . . . then, what about you vacations?' the Policeman asked.

'Annually, we get two months leave, and of course, we are comfortable with that,' the soldier replied innocently.

'Yes . . . but, your wives are not!' the Policeman laughed naughtily. 'Sexual starvation may lead to infidelity . . . poor 'military widows'!'

'Might be'

'If she gets pregnant, how will you tolerate that?'

'Who cares for such silly things?' the Policeman could not believe his ears as the Sardarji replied casually. 'After all, we live in a democratic nation.'

'O.K . . . will you accept them as your own?'

'Surely,' the Sardarji nodded his head.

'Is it? Then, what about their future?'

'Our sons . . . we will put them in the Army. Not even a single job is better than serving the motherland!'

'And, the illegal ones?' the Policeman asked curiously.

'Oh! As usual, they become Policemen'

July 13, 2012

39

DRAMA IN REAL LIFE

'POLITICIANS AND CLERGYMEN NOT allowed,' Gabriel hanged a painted board in front of his home on that Sunday, immediately after Government had announced complete ban on cheap liquor named Arrack. He was so happy to drink Arrack because it was the one and only cheap and safe liquor directly supplied by the Government. Poor man's Scotch! It could give him enough kick just by drinking one quarter! Even though he calls his residence 'home,' his neighbors liked to call it a 'shack or hut'. Whatever it is, Gabriel's peaceful family, including his wife Maria and two careless boys, lived there happily till the ban.

Almost everyone from that fishermen village attended the special mass on that Sunday. Father Silvanos praised the Lord aloud for 'He' made Chief Minister of Kerala, pass orders for the complete ban of Arrack.

'Father . . . Today, you praised our Chief Minister so much . . . But, I would like to ask a very simple question,' Gabriel did seek his permission at the end of sermon.

'Tell me, Gabri'

'If you want to see happiness again in the homes of poor fishermen and other poor-folk, this ban should be lifted as soon as possible,' Gabriel registered his protest.

'Gabri, that's not possible. If you wish to retain the happiness in your home, you should be closer to Jesus . . . You should abstain from liquor . . . This ban is the first step towards that . . . Stepping stone to heaven . . .'

'Then?'

'You see . . . He is going to hike the prices of Indian made foreign liquor soon, by another two hundred percentage . . . Praise the Lord . . . Then, you all will be forced to quit liquor . . .'

'I bet Father . . . If that happens, not even a single family in this village will be happy for ever,' Gabriel marked his protest again.

'Our Lord will find a way out . . . I have faith . . . absolute faith on him . . . Praise the Lord,' Father said with immense happiness.

'I don't have that much faith,' Gabriel said in a pensive mood. 'Father . . . You are staying here happily in this Church . . . But, we wrestle with the Sea day and night. We need cheap liquor to get relieved from our body pains . . . But, how can a man like you, without body pains or any sort of hardships like us, understand us?' Gabriel's Sun tanned dark face started turning red.

'Gabri . . . You are exceeding your limits?'

'What limits?' He went out coolly

'A wayward lamb . . . walks towards the den of wolves . . .' Father thought while keeping the Bible in a safe place.

And on that day Gabriel hanged that painted board in front of his home and stopped attending Church for ever.

'If you don't attend Church, they will not bury your body in our Church graveyard. That's a real disgrace!' Maria tried to revoke his decision by pouring out ancient threats!

'You fool! When this earth is the largest graveyard, I can sleep anywhere! You better throw my dead body to the Sea,' Gabriel shouted.

♥

Maria was sitting there in the market with a huge bucket full of freshly caught fishes. Every bone of her body, she felt, had been aching for millenniums. Being the junior most among the fish sellers, she had to satisfy herself with a lonely stinking corner for her business.

'Maria . . . When did you start fish selling?' I asked in quite astonishment as Gabri never allowed her to go out for fish selling like other women from that colony.

'What to say . . . Gabri doesn't pay us anything now-a-days . . . Whatever he earns . . . that's not even sufficient for him to drink . . . Premji, how can I leave our children?' she said painfully . . . 'Just to get some kick, he is drinking all sort of illicit things . . . He is ready to drink even toilet cleaner . . . Lord . . . please protect his health . . .'

'Don't worry Maria . . . Soon, everything will be O.K.'

'Impossible Premji . . . Government is paying your salaries by looting our pockets . . . the working class . . . They drink . . . None can save them from that . . . Better give them cheap and good liquor'

'Lift the ban? That's what you mean?'

'Yes . . . See now what happens? They are increasing the prices of liquor heavily and reducing the alcohol content too! Purely unethical! My husband is right . . . This is absolute cheating,' she was about to cry.

The riches of the world are made from crystalized tears of women!

♥

'Why didn't you pay your daughter's school fees?' Father Sylvanos asked Samuel, a fisherman under his Church. 'Why don't you support your family now-a-days?'

'It's my money and I know what to do with it . . . Who are you to ask?' Samuel replied Father Sylvanos in excessive anger.

"Father . . . You are losing your grip among your own folk! I warned about this earlier,' Gabriel consoled him with a smile. 'It's the duty of the Church'

'What?'

♥

That Sunday happened to be the second anniversary of the Arrack ban and Gabriel didn't turn his head towards the

Church till that day. Father Sylvanos was very happy to welcome Gabriel back to the Church.

Gabriel was sitting calmly on one of the front row benches inside that small Church. He was sweating like anything as there was a power failure in the morning. The motionless fan, above his head, stooped like his uncertain life. After the Holy Mass, Father Sylvanos started preaching sermon. He told the story of the prodigal son and the entire parish-folk listened to him in pin-drop silence. Maria knew whom he was talking about. And she felt temporary happiness and eternal sadness simultaneously.

Father opened the Bible and started reading aloud Gospel according to Mathew

Mat 17:15 Lord, have mercy on my son, for he is a lunatic and grievously vexed; for oftentimes he falls into the fire, and often into the water.

Mat 17:16 And I brought him to Your disciples, and they could not cure him.

Mat 17:17 Then Jesus answered and said, O faithless and perverse generation, how long shall I be with you? How long shall I suffer you? Bring him here to Me.

Mat 17:18 And Jesus rebuked the demon, and he departed out of him. And the child was cured from that very hour.

Mat 17:19 Then the disciples came to Jesus apart, and said, Why could we not cast him out?

Mat 17:20 And Jesus said to them, Because of your unbelief. For truly I say to you, If you have faith like a grain of mustard seed, you shall say to this mountain, Move from here to there. And it shall move. And nothing shall be impossible to you.

Mat 17:21 However, this kind does not go out except by prayer and fasting.

'My Lord . . . the wayward lamb is back with you . . . Praise the Lord,' Father Sylvanos kept the Bible, closed, on the small table and looked at the calm face of Gabriel.

'Thank you Father . . . You could bring me back to faith . . . Thanks,' Gabriel said in low voice.

Father Sylvanos stood statuesque like Alexander the Great, that too after the conquest of all conquests.

'Father . . .'

'Yes Gabri.'

'Can faith can do wonders?'

'Sure . . . my son . . . That's why you are here'

'Father . . . No need of moving any mountain . . . Just move it a little bit,' Gabriel requested Father Sylvanos while placing a match stick near the Bible on the table.

'Get out . . . you scoundrellllll . . .'

October 04, 2011

40

World Is Blind

Faith . . . What does that mean?

It is a very poignant question, being asked from the very beginning of the social life of human beings. God constructed his worlds, whether material or spiritual, on the strong foundation of faith. Are we missing that now-a-days? Are we trying to break that faith every moment?

From the very beginning of my career in Government service, Ramu was a part of my life and I am very proud that I was his trusted friend. Ramu was our office peon—an embodiment of innocence. He was from very poor backgrounds as his parents belonged to scheduled caste, previously treated as untouchables. His small family comprised of Kausalli: his 'Hitlerian' wife and two boys, almost nearing the end of their teens.

Even though, I had to travel around 120 km, up and down, every-day, I used to be the first man to reach our office in the morning. Ramu was the next guy to reach there.

'Sir, please put a big dot at the centre of my column,' Ramu told while handing over the attendance register. 'I can't see properly . . . from childhood.' He smiled innocently.

'Ramu, you better buy a reading glass'

'Sir, that's very costly'

'Who said that?'

'Kausalli, my wife'

'It costs just hundred rupees . . . You better buy a pair of specs'

'Sir . . . Regularly, I hand over my salary to her . . . She will not spend money for unnecessary things.'

'My God! Then, what will she do with your salary?'

'I don't know . . . Kausalli pays me just . . . enough money for bus fare . . . and for two cups of tea daily,' he smiled again innocently . . . 'Sir, newspaper'

I buried myself deep into the cruelties of news-makers . . . 'A minor girl sexually abused by more than two hundred people . . . Father acts like a pimp . . . Mother spreads the bed rolls.' The female news-reporter introduced the story so spicy; it could give an immediate erection even to an octogenarian! Rotten media bastards . . .

♥

Ramu started his career as a last grade servant during his mid-thirties . . . that too from an educational institution in Cochin (a metropolitan City now) . . . Thousands of naughty students, most of the belonging to rich families, they utilized every opportunity to harass him . . . Mud heads . . . He didn't curse or complain . . .

World remained as blind as ever . . . None knew the pain of his heart . . . Four hungry stomachs, including himself . . . Two small boys and their mother . . . Nothing to eat . . . no home . . . Ramu transformed into the synonym of nothingness! Poor guy was forced to stay in an unused class room where stinking bats were his partners . . . Public works department had been busy constructing a dormitory for people like him in the Moon! (Not yet over!). At last, even his wife was forced to go for work in nearby paddy fields when her younger son started sucking blood from barren breasts.

Krishnan Nair, then time office Superintendent, a kindhearted man himself, showed some personal interest to regularize his appointment. Poor guy was overwhelmed with happiness when he got his salary and arrears, that too after three months of appointment. Within no time, his soul was bathed by the fresh scent of those red notes with denomination of twenty rupees . . . Can it clear the known smell of tears and hunger?

♥

Ramu was capable of defeating Carl Louise, the Olympic Gold medalist, on that special day! He stood there in the post office, panting, with a money order form and post card in hand. But, what is the use? The curved letters on that money order form grinned at him like wild monkeys . . . later they dissolved into thick fog . . . But, God the merciful, appeared before him in the form of a well-dressed Medical representative, with a huge shoulder bag full of sample medicines. He entered into a counter to send some material through registered post.

'Sir . . . Will you please help me to fill this form up?'Ramu requested him.

'Sure,' the gentleman replied in a compassionate voice. 'O.K . . . tell me the address'

'Kausalli, Cheruvayal house, kunnathanam, Kottayam' Ramu felt his voice sweeter than that of anyone. 'Money . . . Rupees six hundred . . . Sir, please write a letter also to her,'he said while handing over the post card.

The gentleman handed over the duly filled money order form and post card. Ramu ran to the nearest hotel immediately after completing the procedures in the post office. Boiled rice, fish curry . . . ahhaa . . . soon, he became the embodiment of taste . . . Later he took half day leave . . . to transcend . . . He slept of peacefully like a new-born . . . The money order receipt fluttered like a butterfly, above his chest in the intermittent gale from his huge nostrils . . . He danced with Kausalli in the evergreen vales of sleep, and that too to the fierce tune of snoring!

Three days later, Ramu saw the last dream of his life . . . Location: an air-conditioned room in Sealord hotel, Cochin . . . Hero: our handsome medical representative . . . Heroin: Saumya, one of the expensive prostitutes of Cochin, nearing voluntary retirement! She too wanted to settle in life! Action: 'DADDY-MUMMY GAME!

Poor Ramu was not all aware of the 'occasionally synonymous' words: 'dream and reality'!

Since then, Kausalli remained his post office, with just only one provision . . . to deposit! Dreaming was also termed as sin!

♥

Heavy rains turned the Solar calendar to July. I noticed a boy, nearing twenty, standing there in the vehicle shed in front our office. He was standing there from the morning. My colleagues were busy standing in the queue to collect their monthly salaries.

'Who is that boy?' I asked Sam, another peon in the office.

'Sir, He is the elder son of peon Ramu'

'Why does he stand there?'

'Don't you know that? He is there to collect his share from his father's salary'

His reply really shocked me.

♥

'Sir . . . Rajendran . . . my elder son . . . he doesn't go for any job . . . he simply moves around with friends, day and night . . . Now, it seems he needs three thousand rupees . . . to buy a big music system . . . with large boxes . . . He loves music . . . But, we need money to thatch the house . . . If I give money, Kausalli will not give me anything to eat . . . Sir, my situation is really bad . . . How can I give him money? He is very angry on me . . . Sir . . . Only rich people can enjoy music,' Ramu opened his Pandora's Box.

'Boys, now-a-days, don't understand the problems and pain of parents,' I said.

'He will kill me . . . Sir . . . He will kill me,' Ramu started crying.

'Ramu, please wipe your tears . . . he will not do anything like that.'

'No, Sir . . . he will kill me some day . . . Yesterday also he told me like this . . . 'I know the shortcut, how you got your job"

'Ramu, will you please elaborate?'

'My father expired while he was working in government service as a last grade servant . . . That's why I got his job . . . they call it 'job on death harness grounds' . . . Sir, he will kill me to get my job,' Ramu was trembling with fear . . . 'I have only two more years of service . . . He will kill me some day . . . he will'

'No . . . Ramu . . . he won't . . . after all he is your son.'

Ramu walked away on his trademark 'slow strides' . . . without even hurting the blades of grass!

♥

Five days later . . . I was discussing some official matter with our Principal in the corridor . . . Ramu ran towards us crying aloud, with his usual bag in hand.

'Ramu, why are you crying like this? What's the matter?' Principal asked.

'Sir, my big brother is no more . . . he passed away, early in the morning.'

'Then . . . why did you come to the office?'

'I have no leave . . . If I take leave, my salary . . . She.'

'Shit . . . O.K . . . You come after three days . . . I will not score your column in the attendance register'

'Thank you . . . Sir.'

'Now . . . run to your home.'

Within seconds, Ramu transformed himself into a happy teardrop . . .

♥

One month passed . . .

'Rhythms of life' . . . I was busy reading the poetry anthology of noted poet Mamta Agarwal . . . What a well-designed book it is! And well written poems . . .

'Affluenza . . . innovative penning, brimming with philosophical astuteness, as well as generous dose of old fashioned cleverity, like the title . . . quite creative': Frank James Ryan Jr.'s comment was there in the back cover. FJR knows the true soul of poetry!

'Mamtaji, who designed this book? It's really beautiful,' I asked her over mobile phone.

'O . . . Thanks Premji . . . It was designed by husband . . . He did a wonderful job for me . . . and that's what husbands are meant for,' she laughed . . .

'Mamtaji, tell me about the sales?'

'Sales? Poetry? Are you joking, Premji? Poetry doesn't sell . . . Poetry doesn't sell at all now-a-days . . .'

Was there deep anguish behind her words? The crest jewel of art is heaped unsold in the dusty racks . . . later dumped into the darkness of warehouses . . . Culture too . . .

My mobile started pestering again . . . Sam was on the line . . .

'Sir, Ramu is no more?'

'Did he?'

'No, Sir . . . It was a heart attack.'

♥

I went to his home on the very next day . . . I don't prefer to watch dead bodies because I like to treasure only their live faces in my mind . . . Rajendran, his elder son, was standing near the fresh grave.

'Rajendran . . . O! What to say?' my voiced chocked . . . 'Anyway he is no more . . . You must find some alternative to look after the home'

'O.K . . . Sir.'

'You come to our office immediately after the ceremonies are over . . . Our principal will move all the official papers in favour of you so that you may get his job . . . Please try to collect his death certificate as soon as possible.'

'Sir . . . I am ready to toil for all life . . . but.'

'But?'

'I don't need his job . . . I don't need,' poor boy started crying aloud . . . 'He told everyone that . . . I will kill him for his job . . . What a punishment Sir . . . what an insult, Sir . . . I don't want his job . . . Some crooked people injected that venom of fear in his mind.'

'O.K . . . Rajendran . . . I can understand your pain . . . But, you have to face real life . . . You have to look after mother and your brother.'

'Sir . . . He was living with hypertension from the very day of his elder brother's death . . . That killed him . . . Not me,' poor boy sank into his knees near the grave.

Only three cents of land . . . Ramu slept there eternally, congested, beside his small home . . .

September 14, 2011

41

The Holy Trail

'Hello . . . Mr. Pai?'

'Yes . . . May I know who is on the line?'

'Sir . . . It's me . . . Premji,' I replied happily, listening to the soft voice from the other end.

'Premji? O! What a pleasant surprise!' He couldn't control the exhilaration

'Sir . . . I am in Bangalore . . . to be very precise, at Lal-Bagh!'

I had been there in Bangalore for the past two days as I was accompanying the annual tour programme of our Automobile Engineering Department students. Being head of the department, I never used to accompany a student's tours. The vigorous students, in their violent teens, vanished into the greenish expanse of 'Lal-Bagh—The Red Garden,' a well-known botanical garden in Southern Bangalore, India.

Annual flower-show was going on in the famous glass house and as a result there was heavy rush in and around the garden.

'The garden was originally commissioned by Hyder Ali, the ruler of Mysore, in 1760 and later finished by his son Tipu Sultan. Lal-Bagh, spanning almost a square km, houses India's largest collection of tropical plants and the rarest plants, has an aquarium and a lake,' a guide started explaining the history of the garden to the tourists standing near the main entrance.

A Maruti Ritz Car stopped next to me and Mr. Pai, a man in the beginning of his fifties, got down. He looked exactly the same as I had met him in the last time. More gray were there in his nearly bald head. He was my Boss, during a short span of three years, when I was working as a sales engineer. We used to travel a lot for the promotion of heavy equipments, especially cranes. He was the first reader and critic of my poems . . . To be very frank, I am free from his influence in life so far . . . He is my great friend and philosopher!

'Hello Mr. Premji,' he shook hands with me . . . 'It has been almost thirteen years since we had met for the last time . . . Am I correct?'

'You are absolutely right . . . Sir'

I got into the car and it sped away to the nearest pub.

♥

'From where did you get my number?' He started the conversation over a mug of chilled beer.

'I searched for the people who deal with the products of 'Escorts construction equipments Ltd.' In Bangalore,'

'That's interesting . . . You are still a salesman!' he laughed.

'You are right, Sir,' I stopped for a second . . . 'You know . . . desperately, I needed a change . . . and that's why I thought of accompanying the students'

'Me too . . . Premji . . . Even I like to be away from the business pressures . . . at least for ten days . . . You know . . . I would love to go the Himalayas'

'To the Himalayas?'

'Yes . . . to the abode of snow . . . to the largest mountain range in Asia separating the plains of India from the Tibetan Plateau . . . I love to feel the clouds as explained by Kalidasa, the great poet . . . Premji . . . will you please join me?'

'I would love to . . . but, unfortunately, I cannot afford the expenses right now,' I replied desperately.

'Expenses? Don't worry about that' Mr. Pai promised firmly . . . 'Let's go to Gomukh,'

It was a word of honour!

♥

It was a fine morning in the middle of May . . . We hired a jeep from Jolly Grant Airport in Dehradun and headed towards Gangotri, 265 km away. Silence encompassed us throughout the journey as we were busy enjoying the scenic beauty of the Himalayan terrains for the first time.

Gangotri, one of the four Hindu religious sites in Utharakhand state of India known as 'Char-Dham,' is dedicated to the Goddess Ganga. Lots of devotees, tourists and Hindu Sanyasins with matted hair were seen everywhere. It is a sleepy town, situated on the banks of the river Bhagirathi, the upper portion of river Ganges on the Greater Himalayan Range at a height of 10,000 feet. We checked in to the hotel where we had our reservations.

♥

It was nearing five thirty in the evening . . . We took bath in River Bhagirathi as a part of holy ritual of the Hindus . . . A single dip was more than enough to convert anyone to an ice-pillar!

I could offer three handfuls of water to the flowing river for the redemption of my beloved grandma . . . She too had the same name as the river: 'Bhagirathi'. She brought the Ganges of happiness to my childhood life, not from the upper heavens, but from her selfless love . . .

'Premji . . . According to the Hindu myths, King Bhagirath did penance here,' said Mr. Pai.

'And after which, heavenly river Ganges came down on Earth as per the wish of Lord Mahadeva . . .'

'To save earth from the fierce impact, Lord Shiva held her in his locks . . . Gangadhara . . . There is no end for the myths' Mr. Pai laughed.

After visiting the Gangotri Temple, later in the evening; we performed Gangaji's arti . . . offering lights river Ganga . . .

'O! Holy Mother . . . please dispel darkness from the universe!' We too prayed along with the large number of devotees coming from all over the world . . .

'O! Holy Mother . . . please take away our sins . . . and enlighten our lives'

♥

The trail to Gomukh starts from Gangotri and the trek starts by entering Gangotri-Gaumukh forest range. It was nearing nine'o clock in the next day morning and there were only a few trekkers on that day . . . Virendar Thapa, our guide in his thirties, arranged permission from the entrance at Kankhu post, 2 Km from Gangotri. He was a very dynamic chap . . . a dare-devil! There were around ten members in our group.

'Earlier, the Gangotri glacier used to start from here . . . Due to melting, now it has gone till Gaumukh,' Virendar Thapa said painfully.

Soon we entered into the rough terrain of horrifying wilderness in the forest area . . . We were so fascinated by the scenic beauty of lush green . . .

'Chidbasa is 9 km ahead of Gangotri,' said our guide.

'Chidbasa?'

'Sir . . . Chidbasa is the abode of Chid trees,' he told us . . . 'Pines'

Though the dusty trail was quite troublesome, we didn't feel any sort of tiredness at all . . . A special variety of Chid trees were seen in mass on the fall in the valley . . . The beauty and intoxicating smell of Himalayan flora is exceptional . . . And at last we reached Chidbasa . . .

We were lucky enough to have tea and some snacks from a small shop in Chirbasa . . . The steaming tea soon turned cold due to the freezing breeze coming out from the faraway glacier . . . And we started heading towards Bhujbasa under the mild Sun . . .

It was nearing two'o clock in the afternoon and we entered into a very difficult trekking zone, approximately three kilometers away from Chidbasa.

'Premji . . . See that . . . ,' Mr. Pai pointed at something.

It was a Bharal, a wild antelope, grazing at the lower-downs and I thought of taking a snap. But . . . I was shocked to see something . . . A loose rock . . . a huge boulder . . . It was on the way down towards us from higher altitudes with massive velocity . . . might be from a height more than 12000 feet . . .

Like two stationary boulders, we both were transfixed there . . . two boulders made of fear! I was so terrified that I couldn't even remember the first line of my daily prayer!

In a quick move, we were pulled back by Richard, a Canadian trekker and we took refuge behind another boulder as per his instruction . . . The fast coming boulder disappeared within seconds to the lower downs! It took away the antelope instead of us! A wild sacrifice!

'Thank you Ric,' I shook hands with Richard . . . 'God's own hands' I pressed his hands tightly out of immense gratitude. The snowy breeze started piercing my panicked lungs without any kindness . . .

'Do you know which place is this?' asked Richard.

'No,' replied Mr. Pai.

'This is Gila Pahar . . . the most dangerous zone in Gangotri-Gomukh trail . . . notorious for the loose rocks falling from the heights and extremely dangerous landslides . . . You know . . . there was a massive landslide on the upper-heights two days back,' said the seasoned trekker in him.

We crossed many shallow streams and wooden bridges . . . By around half past four in the evening, we reached Bhujbasa, 12440 feet above the sea-level . . .

Bhujbasa is the abode of Bhuj trees . . . In the olden times, people used to write on the leaves of Bhuj like present day's paper . . . Kalidasa, the greatest of all poets, wrote his great epics and dramas upon it!

Gomukh, our final destination was only four kilometers away. It could be seen as if in a wide long-shot.

♥

Virendra Thapa quickly established tents for the night stay and soon we could feel the glimmer on the abode of snow . . . It was very difficult for me to adjust with the sleeping bags and other equipment to safeguard oneself from the merciless cold . . .

We got out of the tent as sat upon a boulder . . . O! The lonely Moon, in his majestic brilliance, stood above us like an eternal sentinel . . . and his golden rays added brilliance to the nearby peaks . . .

'Sir . . . sitting outside could be dangerous . . . please take rest inside,' cautioned Virendra Thapa, the guide.

'No problem young man . . . If I am destined to die here, be it so,' replied Mr. Pai while playing a beautiful song from his mobile phone . . .

'Chand jaise mughde pe bindiya sitaraa . . . O sitaaraa . . .'

♥

Early in the next day morning, we started trekking towards Gomukh, closely following Richard, the Canadian trekker.

'This is a very rough trekking rout,' opined Richard . . . 'Very dangerous boulder zone,'

Soon, we were entreated by the majestic view of 'Mt. Shivling,' holy symbol of Shivji, in the western gateway of the lower Gangotri glacier . . . The mighty rays of the morning Sun started sprinkling Gold upon the snow-clad mountain peak . . . And opposite to that majestic 'linga,' stood the triple peaked Bhagirathi Massif . . . The holy peaks were named after King Bhagiratha from time immemorial! We continued our trek paying respect to the serene nature!

'We have trekked almost 18 km from Gangotri' said Mr. Richard.

'Yes . . . we are now at a height of 4255m . . . Sir . . . please watch the wild topography . . . see those boulders and the scattered broken snow . . . O! That's Gomukh!' I cried out.

'Premji . . . just feel the hard clayey snow of the glacier,' Mr. Pai said . . .

♥

Triple peaked Bhagirathi Massif stood behind the terminus like the glittering trident of Lord Shiva . . . The purest water upon earth gushes out from Gomukh, the terminus of Gangotri glacier. It was surrounded by boulders and the sound of water resonated like Omkaar, the all-encompassing primordial sound! River Bhageerathi, the main tributary of Holy Ganges, starts her painful journey from there . . .

'Shivoham . . . Shivoham . . . Shivoham' someone cried out . . .

Gomukh is the holiest place to every devout Hindu.

We walked near the terminus carefully . . . The cold breeze coming out from the glacier was unbearable . . . Mr. Pai collected a handful of water from the turbulent stream and washed his face . . . He sprinkled some drops upon his nearly bald head as if he was in a trance . . .

'Aum Nama: Shivaya' . . . Have mercy upon us . . . O! Lord Shiva . . .

♥

The temperature was less than twelve degrees even in the presence of mild Sun light . . .

We had completed our trek from Bhujbasa to Gomukh just ten minutes back and my lungs were craving for fresh air from the high altitudes, but they were frozen in the multitude of damn-chilled air. I felt somewhat uneasy due to the pressure drop at Gomukh . . .

'Sir . . . I am freezing!'

'Then, what about that guy?' Mr. Pai pointed a man, around seventy, taking bath near the terminus of the Gangotri glacier . . . Gomukh . . .

He was wearing only a loin cloth and I was shocked to watch him taking more dips in the same stream . . .

None can take a dip twice in the same river . . . especially at Gomukh!

Soon, we were befriended by a Major serving in the Indo-Tibetan Border Force. India shares borders with China nearby . . . Himalayas are the divine sentinels of India. Still, we need more protection. He was of my age with family roots in Bangalore. He was so happy to talk with us in Kannada, his mother-tongue.

♥

'That's Naga Swaroopa Baba . . . He won't leave Gomukh even in the toughest of all winters . . . He lives in the nearby caves during rain' said the Major.

'That sounds really strange,' I said.

'He doesn't wander a lot or ask for anything from the tourists . . . And he doesn't even pluck a ripe apple to kill his hunger'

'Then?'

'If somebody gives him something to eat, he eats . . . If a fruit falls from a tree, he eats . . . He sleeps somewhere here on a rock during the nights, that too only in his loin clothes . . . Naga Swaroopa Baba is a man of great spiritual powers,' said the Major with deep admiration towards him as the undertone . . . 'Sab Maa deti hein . . . Holy Mother will provide me everything! That's his unchanged belief!'

I felt really ashamed of watching my Timberland trekking shoes, full sleeved jerkins, monkey caps and every other sort of equipment to protect myself from the cold.

'Is he not afraid of wild animals?' I asked.

'Even I have asked the same question many times! 'I am not the body, but the spirit' . . . That was his simple answer' replied the Major.

'He must be a very happy man,' I said.

'See . . . Major,' Mr. Pai started speaking . . . 'There are thousands of people, like him, living in the Himalayas . . . They call themselves as Sanyasins . . . People doing penance! And the most important thing which I cannot understand is: just by sitting idle like this, what do they contribute to the modern society?'

'Mr. Pai . . . You better ask him directly, the illiterate Baba . . . He is basically a Mauni-Baba—a Sanyasin who observes silence . . . still you can ask him . . . If he likes to answer, he will' The Major walked away swiftly to the nearby Army barracks

♥

Naga Swaroopa Baba was sitting on a rock adjacent to the stream with his body completely covered with ashes, enjoying the one and only luxury of his life: the morning Sunlight! His matted hair and the loin cloth were still dripping wet and his eyes were fixed upon the brilliance of the morning Sun. Might be, he was absorbing energy from the Sun. His frame had the least amount of fat.

'Namaskar Baba,' Mr Pai greeted him politely.

'Namaskar Betaa (son),' replied the Baba in a kinder voice.

'How are you?'

'Because of his mercy, I am fine Betaa,'

'Shall I ask you something?'

'Sure . . . You can . . . Betaa,' the old man encouraged him.

'Baba . . . You are sitting idle always . . . Just by sitting idle, how do you contribute to the modern society?' Mr. Pai asked.

Baba looked into his eyes for a moment and later upon me. His eyes pierced my soul like another trident . . .

'Betaa . . . what is your name?' asked Baba

'I am Mr. Pai from Bangalore and he is Mr. Premji from Kerala'

I could feel the humble pride behind his voice.

'Well . . . well . . . Come and sit here,' Baba invited us . . . 'What do you do, Bete?'

'I am selling very expensive machines' replied Mr. Pai while settling upon the rough rock as if he was trying to glorify himself.

'Very good Betaa . . . Why do you make machines?'

'If you need electricity, you have to make dams. You need machines for the construction of dams . . . You need machines like excavators and cranes for constructing factories, roads, etc and etc, . . . buses, trains, aircrafts . . . everything is a machine . . . we need new machines . . . new inventions to improve the quality of human life,' Mr. Pai poured out his knowledge.

'Betaa . . . How do you construct these machines?'

'Baba . . . we construct the machines using metals'

'Very good Betaa . . . And these metals, where do they come from?'

'Baba . . . these metals . . . they come from the earth'

'Very good . . . And your machines, how do they run?'

'Baba . . . They run on oil and gas'

'Very good Betaa . . . tell me . . . from where does the oil come?'

'Baba . . . Oil also comes from the earth'

'Is it so?' Baba remained silent for a moment . . . 'So, everything comes from the earth! Am I correct, Betaa?'

'You are absolutely right . . . Baba,' replied Mr. Pai.

Soon silence encompassed us. I couldn't avoid looking on to glowing face of Naga Swaroopa Baba in the morning Sun. It was just another brilliant Sun!

'Bete . . . Are you capable of creating a little earth?' Baba broke the silence mercilessly.

We both were shocked to the core!

'No . . . Baba . . . no . . . that's not possible!' replied Mr. Pai, very politely.

'Then, what do you make? What do you invent? Answer me, beloved sons'

Tongue-tied, we sat there like two inert statues made of Ice, before the 'so-called' illiterate man. We were transformed into two amoebas with null ego!

Soon, Baba started talking aloud.

'Bete . . . You didn't invent anything new . . . And you are not going to invent anything newer . . . Everything, that you think—you have invented—were already here . . . And just to make life easier, you construct new machines . . . And ultimately, what do they contribute?'

We both remained silent again.

'They contribute deadly pollution . . . You people are raping the Holy Mother . . . the mother Earth . . . every moment . . . And, by sitting idle here, I am not creating any sort of pollution . . . I am not raping her . . . See . . . What have you done to the river Ganges? How serene is she here' Baba plunged his hand into the holy waters . . . 'You spend billions to clean her . . . every year . . . to make her free from pollution! She knows how to clean herself without even spending a single paisa! Just a single flood is more than enough . . . But, what is the use? You won't leave her again! The rape continues!'

Silently, I looked into the eyes of Mr. Pai. He sat there as if he was in a trance. Baba could puncture our ego with a needle-sharp question forever!

'Bete . . . When you buy a new cloth, you add on to pollution,' Baba continued . . . 'The dyes used for colouring your clothes pollute the soil . . . pollute the water . . . The detergents used for cleaning them, again continue the pollution . . . I own nothing and I am not creating any sort of pollution . . . Bete . . . Whatever Ma . . . the holy Mother . . . gives, I am contended with that . . . If she drops me a fruit, I will eat . . . I am happy with that . . . By sitting idle, I am not creating any sort of pollution! And that is my humble contribution to the modern society . . . And that is my humble contribution to humanity,' Baba stopped talking.

I felt an everlasting lotus bloom within my soul!

'Bete . . . Now also, if you think . . . that I am wasting my life by sitting idle, let it be so,' Baba stopped talking.

We looked into his painful eyes. All I could see was the supreme divine bliss . . . We touched his feet seeking his blessings . . .

'Have peace . . . Bete . . . Do you know what the meaning of Gomukh is?'

'The mouth of a cow,' replied Mr. Pai.

'Earlier . . . might be some hundred years back . . . this snout resembled the mouth of a cow . . . but, What do you see now . . . ? Bete . . . Does it resemble the mouth of a cow?'

We didn't have any answer . . .

'Now, it resembles the mouth of a dragon . . . Earlier the snout was at Gangotri . . . Now it has receded almost eighteen kilometers . . . It was there some hundred years back,' Baba pointed at a little distance—might be around one kilometer . . . 'Everything is getting hotter and hotter . . . you are melting the world away,' he raised his eyes up against the Sun.

♥

'Got the answer?' asked the Major

'Yes,' replied Mr. Pai.

'But, that's incomplete!' said the Major.

'Why do you say so?' asked Mr. Pai.

'Please follow him today,' the Major walked away.

♥

A seventeen year old boy was aiming at rock with plastic bottle in his hand. Unfortunately, the rock was wetted by the turbulent stream from the snout of Gomukh.

'Betaa,' Baba called him from behind and the boy lost his aim.

Baba collected the bottle with the least hesitation upon his face.

'Please do not taint the holy mother . . . Bete . . . especially with plastic' Baba walked away.

The boy was literally ashamed to the core . . .

'Bete . . . you are nothing but water'

Baba was busy cleaning Gomukh the whole day . . . The most serene place on Earth should be kept serene . . . The teenage boy too joined him, might be out of remorse. Huge gunny-bags full of waste plastic and empty bottles were kept behind some huge boulders, unnoticing.

'They will be disposed in Gangotri for recycling . . . Tourism is the worst foe of nature,' opined the Major . . . 'But, one man can make a difference'

'Today, we are going to stay here,' opined Mr. Richard.

Soon, tents were erected near to Gomukh.

We took bath in the stream and collected the purest water ever in two small plastic cans—the pristine waters melting out from an estimated volume of over 27 cubic kilometers of Ice of the Gangotri glacier, about 30 kilometres long and 2 to 4 km wide!

♥

'Baba, we are about to leave' I told him in the next day morning . . . 'We are going to Tapovan'

'You are welcome again, Bete,' he blessed us with open arms.

There must be some specific goal in his life . . . might be something like protecting the holy river Ganges till his last breath . . . What is that?

I felt bit hesitant to walk away . . . and Baba could sense that easily.

'Any more questions? Bete?'

'Baba . . . Everybody has a specific belief or goal to lead his or her life successfully . . . What is your goal in life?'

'Bete . . . I have no specific goals in life . . . I have no craving for money, glory, recognition, food or anything . . . whatever I need to survive, she provides . . . Sab Maa deti hein'

'Then?'

'Only those who are not afraid of death can visit Gomukh . . . Be fearless Bete . . . Be free from the fear of death' he walked away . . .

What's your real name Babaji?

Buddha? Mahaveera? Jesus?

* A story dedicated to the victims of recent Himalayan Tzunami.

June 03, 2013

42

Dream Job

It was a pleasant morning, though it had been raining all night.

'We are having two special guests for today,' I told my wife.

'Don't you allow me to take a little rest during weekends too?' my wife was getting angry as she was reluctant to get up from the bed.

'They are not ordinary people . . . and she will relieve you from the kitchen today.'

'So what?'

'They are eternal lovers.'

'nhum?'

'Yes . . . lovers like us!' I told in her ears and she hugged me tightly.

'Hoo . . . hoo . . . Premji is in love . . . Mummy is in love . . . Mummy is in love,' our little rascals started making noise like naughty dragons roaming in heaven!

'Sleep off . . . you little idiots,' she closed their eyes . . .

♥

Twenty six year old Sandra stood inside the bus shelter, opposite to her working women's hostel, as it was raining cats and dogs. She had been waiting there for at past fifteen minutes and several city buses, going to her destination, had already passed.

'Where is he? It's already nine,' she was getting uneasy . . . 'Idiot . . . Are you on leave today?'

She started scrolling down the contact list in her mobile phone. But, his head appeared from a little distance inside a huge high wind Classic umbrella.

'Rain umbrellas are available in a myriad of styles, colors, shapes, fabrics and sizes. Then, why can't you buy a 'Poppy Nano' four-fold umbrella?' Sandra was getting angry . . . 'Sunny . . . You are not old enough to carry an old man's umbrella cum walking-stick.'

He stepped into the bus shelter, immediately opposite to that where Sandra was standing. He folded the large umbrella with a U-shaped handle and large drops of water started rolling down through the dark fabric.

'Hi Sunny,' she tried to cry out through the rain.

But, he disappeared into his company bus heading towards Technopark, which was also late by fifteen minutes.

♥

'Hey . . . hey . . . stop . . . stop,' she jumped into an auto-rickshaw . . .

'City Center,' she spelled out her destination, a huge shopping mall in the heart of the city.

The vehicle moved so fast, as there was lesser traffic due to rain.

'Sunny . . . you crazy scoundrel . . . I will kill you tomorrow, if you appear a little more lately.' Sandra started giggling uncontrollably.

'Ma'am . . . are you sure, you are heading towards the City Center?' asked the Auto-driver with a smile upon his lips, as he was watching her strange actions through the rear view mirror.

'Yes . . . There is also another mental hospital . . . Are you coming with me?'

The old man shut his mouth forever!

♥

'Sandra, you are late,' said the floor manager . . .

'Please forgive her . . . Ma'am . . . It's impossible to reach here in time today,' said my wife, who is an invaluable customer.

'As you wish, Ma'am,' the floor manager walked away.

'Thanks Ma'am . . . Some fresh varieties of Sarees had arrived . . . Would you like to have a look?' Sandra asked my wife.

'O.K . . . dear . . . you carry on,' I started walking towards the lounge where lot of dailies were heaped on tables.

It was still raining outside and there was no rush inside the mall. My wife called me after half an hour and I joined them for the final selection.

'Sandra . . . your selection is my selection,' I said calmly to provoke my wife . . . 'Please have mercy upon me . . . dear . . . My pocket is almost empty!'

'Done . . . Sir,' she replied happily.

Sandra started folding the Saree*s and blouse pieces carefully. By mistake, a book hidden under the racks fell down.

'What's that?' asked my wife.

'O! Nothing important Ma'am . . . It's a P.S.C guide . . . I would like to have a job at the Government Secretariat and . . . you know, I am dying for it.'

'That's interesting . . . Whenever you get a little break . . .' I said.

'I try to learn something,' Sandra completed the sentence. 'I love to be a 'secretariat assistant,' a wonderful job for the graduates in Kerala.'

'I have a huge collection of questions regularly asked by the public service commission,' my wife liked to extend her kind heart to Sandra. 'They didn't help me in any way! You can use them.'

'O! Thanks Ma'am,' Sandra thanked her out of exhilaration and we started walking towards the counter.

Soon, Sandra could feel the cold bite from the marble floor . . .

'I have to get out here . . . dear Sunny! Otherwise I will have to suffer from rheumatism all life,' she told herself and opened the PSC guide.

*A traditional dress for Indian women.

It was nearing seven in the evening. Sandra saw him getting down from the company bus through the hostel window opening to the street. He started walking towards his home swiftly at it would rain any time.

'He lost it! Haa . . . Ha . . . haa,' Sandra started laughing louder.

'What's wrong with you?' asked Adv. Sumithra, a practicing lawyer at the family court.

'He lost his lousy umbrella . . . ha . . . ha . . . ha.'

'Leave him alone . . . you crazy idiot . . . go and study for your secretariat assistant test,' Adv. Sumithra advised her room-mate like a dutiful elder sister.

'Don't worry Sunny . . . I will gift you a superb 'Poppy Nano' four fold umbrella . . . that you can keep in your pant pocket,' she waved her hands towards him.

His last trace also disappeared in the darkness.

'Tomorrow is Akshaya Tritiya,' said Adv. Sumithra . . . 'It seems, tomorrow is a very auspicious day for buying Gold.'

'Nothing like that Ma'am . . . Corporate owners will invent and publicize such stupid days through national dailies and television channels . . . They know how to be-fool people . . . Akshaya tritiya, this stupid term is only of six years old.'

'And before that?'

'People were more intelligent . . . that's all,' Sandra started laughing . . . 'There will be hell a lot of rush in our shopping complex tomorrow . . . They will buy Gold first . . . and then . . . they will step in for Sarees embroidered with Kasavu, the golden border, next . . .'

'That means . . . you won't even get a single moment to improve your reasoning ability!' opined Adv. Sumithra.

'I am afraid, you are right Ma'am!'

♥

> 'Dear Sunny,
>
> Getting in the rank-list doesn't guarantee a job in the secretariat,' Sandra started writing her daily love letter to Sunny, early in the

> morning. She used to hide it in a place only they both knew in his bus shelter.
>
> I will secure a top rank for you my love . . . Sure, I will join the Finance wing of the Secretariat . . . That's the only reason why I selected Bachelor of Commerce for graduation.
>
> Pray for me dear . . . Please pray for our victory . . .
>
> Love . . . Sandra.'

She closed the pen and started folding the letter carefully. The naughty girl in her wanted to seal it with a kiss . . . but . . .

'O! Sorry dear . . . I didn't brush my teeth.' her face blushed temporarily.

But, to her dismay, she saw him walking down though the main-road towards the bus stop.

'Didn't you see this?' asked Adv. Sumithra . . . 'You examination date has been announced . . . you know . . . it's only two and a half months away.'

'You are right Ma'am.' Sandra went through the daily quite impatiently . . .

'Why don't you take a leave for two months and prepare for it, staying at home?'

'That's unthinkable, Ma'am . . . You know the reason, I hope . . . I have to support my Mom and sister . . . and I am the sole breadwinner.'

'I know . . . I know . . . better than anyone,' Adv. Sumithra replied painfully.

♥

'Hi Sunny,' she waved her hands towards him while getting into her bus on the very next day morning . . . 'Please encourage me . . . Love . . . If you say: 'yes . . . you will qualify' . . . sure I will qualify . . . I have faith on your words, dear Sunny . . . I know, you are always with me . . . Your prayers will always show me the right answers . . . I love you.'

She saw him smiling . . .

'You know . . . Sunny . . . There are only eight hundred vacancies and more than five hundred thousand applicants are there . . . it's really tough . . . be with me, dear friend.'

♥

> 'Dear Sunny,
>
> Exam date is announced. The post of a Secretariat assistant in the finance department is terrific . . . The scope of promotion is just too good . . . I will become the Section officer during my first promotion . . . you know it's a gazetted post . . . I can use green ink! Then, Under Secretary . . . Dy. Secretary . . . Joint secretary . . . Additional Secretary . . . and ultimately Special Secretary to the government . . .

Beyond all, you are my Government . . . I love you, dear Sunny . . . And I promise, I will abstain from every sort of corruption . . . I promise, I will become a government servant who can contribute a large extent for the smooth functioning of the state finance department . . . I will stand for the downtrodden . . .

The syllabus for the objective type questions is quite embarrassing! Will you please guide me to improve my skills in quantitative aptitude, mental ability and reasoning?

Love . . . Sandra.'

♥

'Dear Sandra,

Facing 100 objective questions is not a great thing . . . It becomes great when you are one among half a million applicants and the vacancies are limited! The secret of success is constancy of purpose . . . You can win, my dear . . . You can and you will . . .

Plan your preparations, continue your hard-work . . . Time management is the most important thing . . . You have only seventy five minutes to answer 100 questions. Be careful, while answering questions that you are doubtful, for each wrong answer, one third mark will be deducted.

> And here is my guidance:
>
> Avoid calculators from your life . . . Your mind is the finest calculator ever . . .
>
> Dig deeper, every answer you seek is lying deep buried there!
>
> Believe in your mind and explore the possibilities, your mental ability and reasoning will become razor sharp . . .
>
> Life is the creation of mind, love too . . .
>
> Love . . . Sunny'

♥

'Then, what about general science and current affairs, dear Sunny?'

'Read and re-read! Everything you sense and feel is general science! Try to find out some time to go through the many number of dailies and magazines subscribed in your shopping mall. That will surely improve your knowledge in current affairs . . . And never forget to make notes too!

'That's O.K . . . How can I improve my knowledge about India and Kerala?'

'Please try to love your nation . . . love your state . . . love her people . . . Every secret about them will be opened to your eyes.'

'How can I improve my knowledge about our Constitution and Civil rights?

'Our Constitution is constructed upon the sacrifice of millions of martyrs who fought for our freedom . . . It is your ultimate duty to protect it at any cost . . . You must protect every right of the civil society.'

'How can I improve my general English and proficiency in Malayalam?'

'Anyone from India, who has basic knowledge in his mother-tongue, can learn English within two or three months. But, it is not that easy for a European to learn Malayalam even in a year . . . What do you say?'

'Thanks God! I am good at Computers and Cyber Law . . . Thank you Sunny . . . Thank you so much!'

'Only thanks?'

'Then, what about a flying kiss? O! Dear, you impart me a lot of confidence . . . I love you.'

He walked away happily.

Sandra visited us on the very next morning and soon my sons became personal friends . . .

'Please tell me about your preparations?' asked my wife.

'Goes on as usual.' she replied in a passive manner . . .

'That's not a good sign, dear Sandra . . . I will ask your shop owner to relieve you in Saturdays too . . . She is my personal friend for the past fifteen years,' I said.

'O! Thank you Sir,' replied Sandra.

'Sandra . . . I would like to take you to a special place,' said my wife.

♥

It was nearing four thirty in the evening and Mr. Chakrapani, a retired undersecretary from Accountant General's office was busy reading the literary supplement of 'The Hindu'—the national daily of India in his city home in Nedumangad. He kept a pocketbook and huge dictionary aside to note down the important words and other details picked up from the daily.

'Hello uncle.' my wife greeted her warmly as he is her father's youngest brother . . .

My sons were little reluctant to adjust with the situation and soon they found solace in watching cartoons. After nearly an hour long conversation with him and family, we were about to move to the next destination.

'Sandra . . . you can join us from next Saturday onwards,' said Chakrapani uncle.

'Sir, how much is the fees?' asked the innocent girl.

'Not much . . . That I will tell later.' he replied smiling.

And we dropped her, with a carload of study materials, to her hostel in the evening.

♥

Sandra reached 'Friend's Study Center' at sharp nine in the morning. The training center was functioning inside Government Boys Upper Primary School (BUPS) in the heart of the city. Several young men were busy fixing a huge canvas canopy in front of the school. Some young women started cleaning the ground with long brooms and later they started placing plastic chairs under the canopy. Boys were busy again fixing tube lights around the metal poles as the weather is unpredictable in that hill area. Sandra was virtually embarrassed to the core, watching the unusual set up! By around ten, Chakrapani Master, Director of that study Center appeared in the make shift class room.

'We have a new member today . . . Miss Sandra.' Chakrapani Master said.

She was welcomed into the PSC coaching class, followed by a long clap . . .

♥

Sandra was a bit worried in the evening as she was unable to see Sunny in the morning.

'So?' Adv. Sumithra asked.

'O! Ma'am . . . That's an interesting place . . . More than three hundred students are sitting inside a small tent, that too in perfect silence . . . They all are there with a single aim . . . a government job,' replied Sandra.

'So . . . you like the institution?'

'O! I am in love with it!'

'How was your first class?'

'O! Ma'am . . . Chakrapani Master, the Director of the study center, entered into our class with a single chalk in his hand,'

'No textbooks?'

'No Ma'am . . . He talked for five minutes about the duties of a public servant and later paid homage to the great people departed on that day. Before discussing that day's learning materials, he found out ample time to motivate us, the PSC job aspirants . . . We must be committed to our people.'

'Sounds interesting!'

'Yes . . . Ma'am . . . Everyone has to bring three questions and those will be discussed in the class . . . Some sort of collaborative learning . . . Everybody teaches and everyone learns simultaneously . . . We could cover almost 600 questions in a day.'

'And how much is the fees?'

'Fees? Ha . . . ha . . . ha . . . He teaches us for free . . . It's the commitment of a man to his society . . . !'

'Are there such men alive in our already rotten society?' Adv. Sumithra had a solid doubt!

'Yes . . . Students pay the electricity bills as well as other development expenses for the school.'

'Is he a communist?'

'I think so!' replied Sandra.

♥

Technopark is the first and probably the largest software park in Kerala. Many national and international companies have been functioning there since 1990. She sucks the power of virgin brains and later dumps into debris!

Sunny was having a cup of coffee in the morning, at a cafeteria inside Technopark. He loved the lush green in the huge campus, spanning around five hundred acres.

'Hi Boss . . . Many many happy returns of the day,' Sam, his best pal greeted him in the morning.

'My birthday? How do you know that?'

'Facebook knows everything.'

'Like to have some coffee?'

'Coffee? No way my friend . . . I am going to have at least three pegs on your expense.'

'No way . . . dear Sam . . . I am a tea-totaler . . . Coffee and snacks is more than enough.'

'As you like . . . By the way, you have turned thirty today . . . When are you going to get married?'

'Not yet decided . . . may be in a year or so.'

'I know her . . . Buddy.' Sam started kidding again . . .

♥

The PSC examination was one week away and intensive training programme for the last week had started. And to her luck, the shopping mall remained closed for one week long annual maintenance. The coaching camp was alive all day, spanning from morning eight to evening five, as the school remained closed for ten days.

'Good luck students . . . Please don't do 'night out' tonight . . . Sleep well and face the examination confidently, tomorrow . . . My prayers are always with you . . . You are the winners . . . You are,' Chakrapani Master poured out his supreme blessings to everyone.

'Thank you Sir,' a heavy surge of thanks came out from three hundred and odd powerful lungs . . .

♥

There were so many examination centers throughout the state as it was a statewide examination. Adv. Sumithra accompanied Sandra as her examination center, which was located at around thirty kilometers from their hostel.

The local school was crowded with job aspirants, their friends and relatives. Exam started at sharp two in the afternoon . . . A little girl started crying uncontrollably as her mother was busy rioting with the multiple choice questions inside the school. Her father was in absolute confusion, how to manage the child for an hour . . .

'Hi Sweetie.' Adv. Sumithra called the little girl with a cute smile upon her lips and within no time she jumped into her strong hands.

'It's really embarrassing . . . Usually, she doesn't go with anybody other than her mother,' said the girl child's father . . .

'Managing a child is the toughest task upon earth,' Adv. Sumithra laughed.

'Yes . . . now I come to know that,' replied the young man.

'You naughty!' Adv. Sumithra whispered in her soft ears as the little girl started pressing her firm breasts.

The little girl started giggling . . .

Adv. Sumithra was in cloud nine as she didn't have a child in her fourteen yearlong marriage.

'Here is the answer key,' Adv. Sumithra showed her the last page of Mathrubhumi daily . . .

'Please check it with your answers.'

'There is no need for that, Ma'am.' replied Sandra.

'You mean?'

'I will be one in the first two hundred ranks,' she said confidently and firm belief was absolutely right.

♥

It was a fine Sunday and classes had already started at Friend's Study Center. Chakrapani Master was busy dealing his daily routine, discussing questions and their answers with three hundred odd students.

'Sir . . . ,' Sandra called him softly.

'Hello Sandra . . . Please come in,' he welcomed her.

'Sir . . . Please,' she handed over her appointment order to his feeble hands, knelt down and touched his feet for blessing. 'Bless me.'

A drop of tear fell upon her head . . .

'Sandra is going to join the Finance Department as a secretariat assistant, tomorrow . . . ,' announced Chakrapani Master. 'I welcome Sandra to share her experiences.' He handed over the microphone to her.

'As my friend Sunny used to encourage me, I would like to encourage you all through his own words . . . The secret of success is constancy of purpose . . . and I am thankful to all of you . . . especially Chakrapani Master . . . I got a job . . . but, that doesn't mean, I am away from you all . . . I will come here whenever I am free . . . And certainly not empty-handed, but with a bunch of newly found questions . . . We will fight it out . . . dear friends . . . we will . . . Thank you,' she handed over the microphone to Chakrapani Master as her lungs started chocking . . .

♥

Government Secretariat was another strange world to Sandra . . . One has to deal with the ministers, MLAs, officers, politicians and the public there. Her previous sales experience in the shopping mall helped her lot to manage them all without any complaint.

'Are you a Roman Catholic or Latin Catholic?' asked the section officer on the third day of her joining.

'Why Ma'am?' asked the innocent girl in her.

'Another secretariat assistant had enquired about you . . . Usually, almost everyone works here, finds partners also from here . . . You know, there are not much transfers . . . I too am not an exception,' she replied smiling . . .

'That's an interesting piece of information . . . Ma'am, I am a Human Catholic!'

That ended up in a huge laughter . . .

'Do you like him?' she pointed a handsome guy standing out in the corridor.

It was nearing quarter to nine in the morning and she waited for Sunny in his bus shelter. Six or seven people were also standing there for quite some time.

'There might be some traffic block,' opined an old man among them . . . 'They have fixed many traffic signals at unwanted places.'

'There are possibilities . . . ,' said his wife.

Wonderful couple, that too in this ripe age,' Sandra felt an unknown happiness bubbling out from deep within.

Sunny also joined the crowd quietly and he looked into his watch quite impatiently.

'Sunny,' Sandra called him from nearby . . . 'A gift for you.'

She showed him a brand new Poppy Nano four fold umbrella.

'Sunny? Who is Sunny? Ma'am . . . you are mistaken,' objected the young man . . .

'I love you Sunny . . . and I will marry 'only' you,' Sandra poured out her heart.

'No . . . I am not Sunny,' he said louder.

'I have seen many guys like him, cheating young girls,' the old woman started shouting.

'They act like dumb characters later,' the old man started supporting his wife blindly.

'Call the Police,' shouted the old woman . . .

'Ma'am . . . please don't do that.' Sandra tried to please the old woman . . . 'Please.'

But, she was helpless as the situation started growing wild.

♥

'Please drive faster . . . I don't want to get trapped into another traffic jam,' my wife started eating my brains again.

'O.K . . . then, you drive,' I was about to pull over out of anger.

'Hey . . . hey . . . please pull over there . . . I think Sandra is in trouble.'

I stopped the car next to the bus shelter and my wife jumped out.

'What's wrong dear?'

'Nothing Ma'am.'

'There is something really important . . . This guy abused her royally and he pretends he doesn't know her.' said the old woman in between.

'Is it Sandra?' my wife was getting angry.

'Premji Sir . . . please help me to get out of here,' asked the young man.

'So, you know him?' my wife was getting angrier and this time her victim was me!' I hate your bad company, now-a-days,'

'Get in the car,' I told him stubbornly and he followed my order happily.

'You too get inside.' my wife told Sandra . . .

'He might be a policeman,' the old woman opined about me when we were about to drive away.

♥

I stopped the car near an empty park in the city.

'Everyone . . . please get out.' I switched off the roaring heat engine . . . 'Now . . . tell me . . . what is your intention?'

'Sir . . . I have no intentions,' said the young man.

'And what about you, Sandra?' asked my wife.

'I didn't have any intentions since last week . . . But,' Sandra stopped in the middle.

'Please tell it clearly.' my wife forced her to pour out her mind.

'Ma'am . . . You know everything about me . . . and you both helped me a lot . . . Ma'am . . . I wished to secure a job in the government secretariat . . . And I wanted someone to encourage me every moment to realize my dream . . . an imaginary lover . . . and I named him 'Sunny' . . . I wrote many letters to him and he replied with care . . . I wrote the replies for the sake of him too . . . He helped me to realize my dream . . . And that someone is he.' Sandra pointed towards the young man.

'This is absolute madness,' the young man said . . . 'O! Gosh! I am not Sunny!'

'You could have left him along with your victory . . . Everything would have been alright by then,' I said.

'I tried it out desperately . . . Sir, then only I could understand . . . that I am madly in love with him . . . He has become an obsession to me.'

'Really embarrassing!'

'How can I leave a man, who is the sole owner of my heart? I cannot escape from him all life . . . I can't . . . I can't.' Sandra stopped talking while looking into his eyes and the poor man sank into the park bench.

'Do you have any idea about him?' I asked Sandra.

'No . . . Sir.'

'He is not a government employee like you . . . He is a low-paid, temporary, generator operator at Technopark . . . He lives with his mother in a small rented house and she is bedridden for the past three years . . . His life is not that attractive as his handsome outlook,' I tried to inform her.

'Sir . . . I am not bothered at all.' Sandra replied boldly and her serene beauty had almost doubled on that particular moment.

'Get up young man . . . I really envy upon you . . . Life is a silly game . . . But, the players must pay heed to the laws of love . . . Good luck . . . My friend.' I shook hands with him and started walking towards the car.

'To love is human; to be loved is divine,' my wife told the young man . . . 'Be blessed . . . man and woman.' She joined their hands and started walking towards the car.

'Where are we going?' my wife asked when I took an unexpected left turn . . . 'We will miss my cousin's marriage . . . you know it's already late!'

'Tell him to get lost . . . We are going to act in a love song . . . all alone . . . at home.' I stared humming an old tune.

♥

She too sat with him on the park bench and they didn't speak anything for the next five or six minutes.

'Sunny,' she broke the silence.

'nhum'

'Please tell me your real name?'

'My name is love!'

July 07, 2013

Contact: premjipremji@live.com